# THE MAVERICK

## BY

## RHONDA NELSON

**MILLS & BOON®**

*Pure reading pleasure*

*All the ch*
*imagination*
*bearing the*
*by any indi*
*incidents ar*

*All Rights*
*in part in a*
*Harlequin E*
*any part the*
*or by any m*
*recording, s*
*without the*

*This book is*
*trade or other*wise, *be lent, resold, hired out or otherwise circulated*
*without the prior consent of the publisher in any form of binding or*
*cover other than that in which it is published and without a similar*
*condition including this condition being imposed on the subsequent*
*purchaser.*

*First published in Great Britain 2007*
*by Harlequin Mills & Boon Limited,*
*Eton House, 18-24 Paradise Road, Richmond, Surrey TW9 1SR*

*ISBN: 978 0 263 85595 1*

*14-1107*

*Harlequin Mills & Boon policy is to use papers that are*
*natural, renewable and recyclable products and made from*
*wood grown in sustainable forests. The logging and*
*manufacturing processes conform to the legal environmental*
*regulations of the country of origin.*

*Printed and bound in Spain*
*by Litografia Rosés S.A., Barcelona*

## RHONDA NELSON

A bestselling author, past RITA® Award nominee and *Romantic Times BOOKclub* Reviewers Choice nominee, Rhonda Nelson writes hot romantic comedy for the Blaze® line. In addition to a writing career, she has a husband, two adorable kids, a black Labrador and a beautiful bichon frisé who dogs her every step and frequently cocks his head in utter bewilderment at her. She and her family make their chaotic but happy home in a small town in northern Alabama. She admires the honourable qualities in our men in uniform, but is secretly thrilled by the occasional bad boy, as well.

For my son, who is too young to read this,
but already possesses the finer qualities
of the heroes featured in this series.
I love you, little buddy. This one is yours.

# *Prologue*

*LOSING HIS TOUCH, HELL,* Colonel Carl Garrett thought, mortified by the vicious rumor. He scowled and watched the antique pocket watch—General Robert E. Lee's no less—suspended from his index finger spin slowly in midair. He hadn't spent the past thirty-three years in the military and received his most recent commendation for meritorious service only to be ushered out to pasture to make way for up-and-coming wannabes, dammit.

*Him? Retire?*

He was certainly old enough, of course, and his wife periodically asked when he planned to hang up his hat, so to speak, but Garrett simply couldn't wrap his mind around being…useless. No longer being of value. His days were filled with purpose, a noble one he'd been proud of from the first moment he'd entered the service, as a wet-behind-the-ears punk with more attitude than sense. The military had thrashed some sense into him, had given him a goal and a dream and the idea of letting those go, of puttering around his greenhouse or trailing along behind his wife at the grocery store was simply...excruciating for him.

The murmurs and rumors of his imminent retirement—a retirement he neither planned nor wanted—had started immediately following his commendation. In retrospect, Garrett realized now he should have seen it for what it was—a nice career ender, the cherry on top of the sundae.

While he knew he commanded the respect of the majority of his peers, he also knew there were a few people around here who wished that he'd move on and make room for new blood. Naturally, one didn't get to his level without making a few enemies. But the idea of doing that was as out of the question now as it had been the first time the issue of his retiring had come up.

Garrett wasn't finished yet. He still had work to do. And to prove that he was as every bit as sharp as he'd always been, he had something up his sleeve. And that something was sitting right outside his office—impatiently, of course, and most likely annoyed and bitter as hell—right this very minute. The thought drew a smile, one of few he'd managed over the past few weeks.

Guy McCann—his maverick.

In all of his years in service, Garrett had never met a man with better instincts and the balls to follow them, no matter how risky the move might be. And when it came to instilling confidence and leading a team, Guy McCann had been the best of the best. He'd led Project Chameleon, one of the most respected covert operation special forces units the army had ever known, on more than two dozen highly dangerous missions—and had been successful each and every time, an unparalled record.

His days of service were over, of course, but if McCann could teach this new team Garrett had put together a fraction of the skill he possessed, then that would put an end to the rumors that he'd lost his touch.

The proof was in the pudding, so to speak, and Garrett was counting on McCann to whip up something special.

Given McCann's present state of mind, it might not be the most prudent move for Garrett to put his faith in the troubled former Ranger. But like McCann, there were times when a man simply had to follow his instincts, and each and every one of Garrett's told him that McCann needed to fulfill this favor just as much as Garrett needed him to be successful.

Garrett scowled, thinking of the coming confrontation. It was a pity they were about to get off to such a bad start.

# 1

*PECKER FILETED WITH a butter knife.*

*Balls removed with flaming pinchers.*

*Starving hyenas feasting upon his privates.*

And those were the least gruesome scenarios of what Guy McCann would rather be facing—or more accurately where he'd rather *be* at the moment, he thought with a smirk as he waited impatiently in Colonel Carl Garrett's outer office.

*Fort Benning, Georgia—the last damned place on God's green earth he'd ever wanted to be again.*

Though there was absolutely no true humor in the situation, he chuckled darkly anyway. A grenade of nausea sat in his gut, threatening to detonate and his entire body vibrated with the need to flee—to be anywhere but here. It was too much. Too hard. Regret, failure and grief twisted his insides until his fists involuntarily clenched and he squeezed his eyes tightly shut, forcing away the image of his fallen friend.

*Danny Levinson. Killed in action. His fault.*

Guy released a small breath and massaged the bridge of his nose. While other people gazed across the beautiful grounds of Fort Benning and saw a rolling landscape dotted with enormous old trees, Guy only saw…hell. His own personal variety, because being here was like being plugged directly into the worst part of himself.

The last time he'd sat outside Garrett's office it had been to barter for his freedom. He'd thought at the time that he'd be willing to pay any price, would grant Garrett any favor—the colonel's fee for pushing their clearance papers through.

He, Jamie Flanagan and Brian Payne—his friends and Project Chameleon comrades— had been involved in an off-base brawl that could have held them up indefinitely. And considering that the army had tried every way in the world to get the three of them to rethink leaving the military to start with, Guy had to admit that they'd handed the top brass the perfect opportunity to make that happen. Garrett had pulled a hat trick and for that he would be forever grateful.

Grateful enough—grudgingly, of course— to even come back here for a week. As an instructor, no less.

But it was only a week he reminded himself. Actually, less. Five days. He blew out a breath. Five miserable days, then the rest of his life would be his own and he could return to Ranger Security—his post-military career choice—a free man. Not free from the guilt, of course. He'd never get past that, wouldn't allow himself the luxury. But free from Garrett and the military, at any rate.

It was a start, however feeble.

"The colonel will see you now," Garrett's secretary said, startling Guy out of his unpleasant reverie. He nodded briefly at her, then stood and strode into Garrett's inner sanctum.

An impression of power and the strangely comforting scent of cherry tobacco greeted him the instant he entered the room. Garrett sat behind a large gleaming desk, but found his feet and extended his hand as Guy approached.

Despite Garrett's choice in their favors— Jamie had been sent to Maine under the impression that he would be guarding the colonel's granddaughter only to arrive and discover that he was supposed to seduce her away from another man, and Payne had been dispatched to Gettysburg, the object of a bet, to retrieve a pocket watch which had been rumored to have belonged to General Robert E. Lee—Guy had nevertheless always had the utmost respect for Garrett. He was a patriotic old warhorse whose piss-and-gravel voice had been honed on the battlefield, then later respected in the boardroom.

Furthermore, only a hell-raiser could recognize another hell-raiser and Guy had caught that reckless fuck-you identifying spark in Garrett's sharp blue eyes the instant he'd first looked into them more than four years ago.

"So, how does it feel to be back?" Garrett asked, his face wreathed in a knowing smile.

"It sucks."

Garrett chuckled. "Blunt as usual, I see."

"Blunt works." He settled himself in one of the chairs positioned in front of Garrett's desk. "It doesn't leave much room for misunderstandings."

His expression remained bland. "It would serve you better if it were tempered with a little tact."

True, Guy conceded with a small shrug, but tact had never been his style. He'd walked on eggshells around his miserable old man until he'd gotten big enough to fight back. At that point he and tact had parted ways and Guy didn't give a damn if they ever reunited. Wit, strength, luck and his ability to never mince words had served him well over the years. Being of the if-it-ain't-broke-don't-fix-it school of thought, Guy wasn't interested in changing the status quo. The world could accept him for who he was or go to hell. It was as simple as that.

"I'm not here to receive a lecture on tact," Guy told him. "I'm ruining your Sunday—and Gladys's—" he added, jerking his head toward Garrett's secretary in the outer office "—because I'm here for instructions. I'm assuming you've got them?"

Garrett leaned back in his chair and scowled, his brushy brows forming an intimidating line. "If it's all the same to you, McCann, I'll set the pace for this meeting. You'll get your instructions in due time." He paused. "As it happens, we're waiting on someone and I'd just as soon not have to repeat myself."

A chill landed in Guy's belly and all his senses went on alert. He arched a brow. "Waiting for someone?"

Garrett picked up a small crystal paperweight and carefully polished it on his sleeve. "Yes."

When he failed to elaborate, Guy exhaled

an irritated breath and asked the obvious question. "Who?"

"Julia Beckam."

The name didn't ring any bells of recognition, but for whatever reason, a warning sounded instead. And that was ridiculous, dammit. It was merely a name, that of the feminine variety, admittedly, but just a name all the same. Guy gritted his teeth, waiting for Garrett to supply further information.

Naturally, he didn't.

"Who exactly is Julia Beckam?" Guy asked tightly.

Garrett looked up. "She's your co-instructor."

A premonition of dread sent a wash of cold chills over his suddenly hot skin and his first instinct was to leap from his chair, tell Garrett to go to hell and leave Fort Benning so fast it would make the world spin in the opposite direction. Images of his newly shackled and affianced friends loomed largely in his mind, no small wonder considering they'd been taunting him with predictions of falling in love on his mission for Garrett, as well.

Ironically, both Jamie and Payne had found the love of their lives while repaying their favors. To make matters worse, he'd not only taken a ribbing from his smug friends, but had been forced to listen to their significant others—Audrey and Emma—gleefully ooh and goo over how fabulous it would be to see the wind knocked out of Guy's sails.

Or more to the point, find him anchored with a ring around his finger.

Like hell.

A tornado of rage swirled around his brain, making it difficult for him to speak without growling. "I wasn't aware that I had a *co*-instructor."

Garrett actually smiled at him. "How would you know when I hadn't told you yet?"

Feeling every muscle in his body atrophy with anger, Guy shifted forward in his seat. "I think you've mistaken me for Payne," Guy said, his voice lethally controlled. "Duty has never been my strong suit. I will not be misled like Jamie, nor lied to like Payne. In fact, you can safely assume that unless you level with me completely, right now, then favor or not, I will walk out of here and you'll play hell ever getting me back. I owe you. I know that." He shot Garrett a hard look. "But I will not be manipulated."

A beat slid to five while Garrett considered him. "The only manipulation I'm guilty of is leaving Ms. Beckam's involvement in this training session a mystery to you," he finally said, evidently opting to take Guy's threat seriously. It was a good decision, Guy thought, since he'd been fully prepared to back it up.

"And you did that because?" Guy prompted.

Garrett shrugged. "Would you have come if I'd told you that a female relationship therapist would be teaching alongside you?"

"Hell, no," Guy replied quickly. A relationship therapist? He snorted. "You've paired me up with a shrink?"

"She's a therapist," Garrett corrected. "The

daughter of an old friend of mine and she's at the top of her field. Recent studies suggest that the dynamic between teams and couples share many of the same facets. Trust, of course, being the most important in both. A spouse who doesn't trust or respect a partner leads to trouble. It's the same scenario with our special forces teams. You know that. If you don't trust the guy who's giving the order, if you don't respect him, what happens?" Garrett pulled a face. "Everything goes to hell in a hand-basket. The chain of command is broken."

He knew all about that, Guy thought, jerked back into a memory he desperately didn't want to explore. *Gunfire, the spray of sand, then Jamie topping the hill, Danny hanging limply in his arms.* The image was permanently etched into his brain, almost as though it had been tattooed there.

It was the moment—no, the instant—that life as he'd known it had forever been changed.

He'd gone from being a badass Ranger with a penchant for bending the rules just shy of the breaking point to a brokenhearted friend who no longer deserved the respect of his peers.

And trust? Sweet God. It was laughable. Garrett wanted him to teach other men how to trust each other when he no longer trusted himself? When it was Danny's misplaced trust that had landed him in Arlington? Hell, he was the last damned person who should be teaching this particular subject. How on earth Garrett had failed to grasp that concept was out of Guy's immediate understanding. The colonel wasn't ordinarily so thick.

Did he see the similarities between couples and teams? Certainly. But that didn't mean he wanted to share the floor with a bonafide romantic—and she'd have to be to be in her profession, right?—and listen to her lecture about getting in touch with "feelings" and "emotions" and all that other crap.

He swallowed a roar and felt a tick develop near his right eye.

Garrett paused, and seemed to be weighing

his words. "The team which you will be instructing is Project Chameleon's replacement, McCann. You are aware of the nature of the job, you know what's at stake. It's imperative that this team comes together well and is equipped with every necessary advantage I can give it. Presently, the benefit of your expertise and experience offers the best hope for its success. I realize that you don't want to be here, but for the sake of the men I'm going to entrust into your care for the next few days, I'm counting on you to use some of that legendary skill for their benefit."

Bloody hell. Project Chameleon's replacement team? *That's* who he was working with? He stifled a helpless laugh. Mother of God—

The door opened and Gladys peered into the room. "Ms. Beckam has arrived," she said.

"Good," Garrett told her. "Send her in."

Because he didn't appreciate the bomb Garrett had just dumped in his lap, or the colonel's tactics and maybe just because he was an ass, he neither stood nor even turned around in his seat to acknowledge Julia Beckam's presence. It was rude and unconscionable and completely against his very nature—not to mention his mother would pinch the living hell out of him for being so disrespectful, but Guy was annoyed past caring.

Furthermore, now seemed like the perfect time to let Garrett and Ms. Beckam know that he was nobody's lapdog. He was still here because he *chose* to be here and if at any time he changed his mind, he'd bail.

End of story.

Evidently realizing that Guy wasn't going to be a gentleman, Garrett shot him an irritated look, then stood and rounded his desk. "Ms. Beckam," he greeted warmly.

"I apologize for being late," said a beautiful, almost smoky-sounding voice. "I was… unavoidably detained."

The slight irritation he heard in her voice immediately begged the question "By what?" but since he'd cast himself in the roll of insufferable ass, he could hardly turn around now and probe, could he?

"No, problem," Garrett assured her. "Former Lieutenant Colonel McCann and I were just catching up."

He felt her gaze, sensed her hesitation. Finally she said, "Well, shall we get started?"

"Certainly." Garrett found his place behind his desk once more and Guy felt Julia Beckam move into the seat next to him. A flash of static seemed to crackle around him, making him shift in his chair and a cloud of honeysuckle settled over him. It reminded him of hot, humid summers. Of home, on the very rare occasions it had been good. From the corner of his eye, he caught a glimpse of a long shapely leg peeking out from a navy skirt.

*Shit.*

Another glimpse revealed the outline of a very plump breast beneath a white silk button-up blouse. He mentally groaned and felt the room shrink.

*Double shit.*

Clearly a glutton for punishment, Guy finally turned to glance at her and, if the sight of her leg and breast had made the room shrink, then one look at her uncommonly beautiful face made it tilt. He experienced a violent hot flash immediately followed by a quaking chill and his stomach did an interesting dive the likes of which he'd never felt before. A shot of adrenaline burst into his bloodstream and instantly headed for his groin.

High cheekbones, full pouty mouth, a nose that was a little too large for her face, but seemed to fit anyway and eyes the shade of a new leaf made her one of the most alluring creatures he'd ever set eyes on. She wore little to no makeup and her hair, though pulled back in a severe schoolmarm knot at the back of her head, was a pale blond the shade of sunlight. The hairstyle and the clothes might have said "Take me seriously," but the face and the body screamed an abbreviated version— "Take me."

As though she'd somehow read his mind,

her lips formed the slightest hint of a chilly smile. "Mr. McCann."

Guy grinned and inclined his head. "Ms. Beckam."

The pleasantries over, Garrett moved into colonel mode and outlined what he expected of them. He handed a class outline to each of them. "As you can see, McCann will be in charge of the team-building aspects of the curriculum and Ms. Beckam, we'd like you to focus on the emotional benefits of building a trusting relationship." He smiled. "These teams need to feel married in all but the biblical sense."

Julia pulled a pair of reading glasses from her purse and perused the documents. There shouldn't have been anything remotely sexy about that, but for whatever reason, Guy felt his dick get hard all the same. He squirmed and rolled his eyes.

Clearly it was past time he got laid.

"The two of you can get together and decide which exercises and lectures will compliment the other. In essence, you're a team, as well."

He slid a look at McCann and offered a pointed smile. "Might I suggest getting better acquainted over dinner?"

Startled, Julia looked up. Her gaze darted nervously between Garrett and himself and it was quite obvious that the idea of sharing a meal with him wasn't what she'd like to do at all.

Which was probably why Guy grinned broadly at her and heard himself say, "That sounds like an excellent idea."

Julia smiled weakly, but didn't say anything.

"Wonderful," Garrett said, evidently pleased. "For lodging, please check in at Olson Hall and they'll get the two of you fixed up. Gladys has called ahead, so they're expecting you."

"Is that everything?" Guy asked.

"For now," Garrett told him. "I'll be checking in to see how things are going." He glanced at Julia. "Ms. Beckam, if you have any questions feel free to give me a call. However I think that McCann will be able to field most inquiries. He's familiar with the way things are run here on post."

Julia nodded, shot Guy another one of those looks which said she doubted the credibility of that claim. For whatever reason, Guy got the distinct impression that she'd taken his measure and found him lacking.

It wasn't the usual reaction he normally received from women—he didn't have to beat them off with a stick, exactly, but a smile and a wink usually did the trick. Could it be that she was the exception to the rule? He slid her a brooding glance, intrigued beyond reason. Stranger things had happened.

Julia stood and shook Garrett's hand. "Thank you for this opportunity, sir. I think you'll be pleased with the results."

Garrett smiled. "I'm counting on it."

Guy acknowledged Garrett with a nod of his head, then followed Julia Beckam out of the colonel's office. She walked ahead of him without sparing him so much as a backward glance. Tit for tat? he wondered. Or was she simply that rude?

Time to find out.

"Do you know where you're going, Ms. Beckam?" Guy drawled.

She turned and shot him a wry look over her shoulder. "No, but I have a map of the area in my car and, being as I'm neither blind nor stupid, I think I can figure it out." She turned back around, purposely, it seemed, dismissing him.

Both then, Guy decided, scowling. "How about I make it easy for you and you follow me?"

She didn't bother looking at him. "Very chivalrous, but no thank you." Chilly sarcasm hung like icicles in her voice.

What the fu—? "Do you need help getting that thing out?"

This time she did turn toward him, looking thoroughly perplexed. "What thing?"

Guy smiled sweetly at her, provoked past his normal limits. "The stick up your ass. I imagine it's uncomfortable."

A fleeting flash of hurt clouded her gaze, then she blinked and the usual chill emerged. She deliberately retraced her steps. "Let's get something straight. I am perfectly aware of the fact that you don't want to work with me. You made that abundantly clear the instant I walked into Colonel Garrett's office." She rolled her eyes, made an exasperated huff as though mystified and repulsed by the workings of the male brain. "I'm treading on your precious male territory, or ruining your 'manly' team-building exercises with my touchy-feely approach to trust bonding and you'd just as soon not work with me." She pinned him with a glare. "Well, newsflash, buddy. As shocking as it might be, I don't particularly want to work with you, either, but it's a necessary evil and I've accepted it. I suggest you do the same."

"*When* did you accept it?" Guy asked as a horrible suspicion rose.

She blinked, her tirade derailed. "Two weeks ago when Garrett informed me that I'd be working with you."

Guy smirked at her. "Newsflash," he said sarcastically, throwing the phrase right back at her. "I found out I'd be working with you two minutes before you walked into the room. I haven't had time to 'accept it' yet."

She paused, her clear green gaze considering and something about that look made him feel distinctly uncomfortable. "Now that's interesting."

"What's interesting?" Guy asked, unnerved by that probing I-know-something-that-you-don't look.

She cocked her head and an infuriating little grin turned her lips. "That Garrett's put a guy he clearly doesn't *trust* in charge of a trust-building class. Irony, I wonder," she mused annoyingly. "Or something else."

And with that parting shot she turned and walked away, leaving him to wonder, as well.

About her.

# 2

PUT THAT IN YOUR PIPE and smoke it, you great ass, Julia thought as she made her way back out to her car. She consulted her map and aimed her car toward Olson Hall. To her chagrin, Guy McCann fell in behind her, then had the audacity to smile and wave when he saw her checking out her rearview mirror.

Good grief, the man was insufferable.

In her line of work she was used to dealing with men who'd been dragged against their will into her office by their significant others, had fought prejudice and preconceived notions by thick-headed, cocky blowhards for as long as she'd been in business.

So the minute that Colonel Garrett had told her that she'd be sharing a workshop with a former Ranger, she'd known—*known*—that there'd be trouble. She'd fully expected him to be a cool, sarcastic condescending he-man whose new goal in life was to make her feel small and foolish. She'd imagined him all but pissing in the corners of the room, marking his territory.

What she hadn't counted on was him being so damned good looking.

And for reasons she could not begin to explain or even understand that absolutely *infuriated* her. She frowned. Insult to injury, she imagined, given the weekend she'd had.

Guy McCann was one of those genuine baby-I-can-rock-your-world bad boys whose charm and irreverence made him all the more irresistible. Bright green eyes, a cool smooth jade, danced with equal measures of intelligence and wickedness and an open invitation to sin that made a girl's pulse inexplicably leap. And while his smile might have been crafted by a divine hand, it had been honed to perfection by the devil because she'd never seen anything so carnally sinful.

Exceptionally high cheekbones, a firm angular jaw and a dimple in his right cheek made him all the more appealing. Add a shock of untidy jet-black hair and a body built on David's scale—even slouched carelessly in his chair, she'd been hammeringly aware of that fact—and he became downright lethal.

A simple *sexy* didn't begin to cover it.

In short, he was the kind of guy who could charm the pants—and everything else—right off a girl, make her think it was her idea, then cut her loose without realizing that she'd just had her heart crushed beneath his cocky heel. And the instant he crooked a finger and that smile again, she'd get in line for guaranteed misery once more.

Ugh…sickening.

He was trouble with a capital *T* and if she had a brain in her head—particularly given her present frame of mind and her newest personal revelation—she'd drive her car right off this base and hightail it back to Atlanta.

Unfortunately, in light of recent mortifying events, Julia had no desire to go home at the moment. When she'd told Garrett that she'd been "unavoidably detained" that had been a mild understatement.

In truth, she'd been in jail.

She, who'd never had so much as parking ticket, *incarcerated*.

Renewed mortification stung her cheeks and she swallowed tightly. Julia still had a hard time making it process, still couldn't believe that things had gone so terribly wrong. In an effort to revive another flatlined relationship, she'd gone to extreme measures.

Or at least they had been for her.

"Variety," Warren had said, Julia remembered now, angered once again. He'd wearied of their "vanilla sex life" and longed for something a little more titillating, a request she'd heard from previous boyfriends, as well.

When confronted with a problem, Julia was

the type to address it head-on. If Warren's complaint had been the first that she'd heard, then she merely would have chalked it up to it being simply his opinion, not the consensus. But as this was the *third* time she'd been accused of being too tight in the sack, Julia knew that, sadly, *she* was the problem.

Gallingly, in the bad sex department, she was the common denominator.

Since Warren had expressly asked for variety, Julia had researched a few scenarios and decided that role-playing wouldn't put her too far out of her comfort zone. Knowing that Warren would be returning from a business trip late last night, she'd decided to surprise him. She'd applied makeup à la hooker, donned a long red wig and a sexy leather dress with a built-in push-up bra, then had driven over to Warren's house for a night of chocolate sex in which she hoped she would finally reach climax. So far, just like his predecessors, Warren had managed to trip her trigger digitally…but never during sex. More proof that there was something wrong with her, Julia thought with a small despondent sigh.

At any rate, she'd parked several houses farther down his block so that he wouldn't see her car, then had hurriedly backtracked to his house.

At this point, things had gone terribly, terribly wrong.

She'd fumbled the keys into the bushes, then had scrambled around in the dark in a vain attempt to find them. Ten minutes later, wig askew and runs in her micro-fishnet hose, she'd given up and decided to resume her search in the morning. Locked out of the car, Julia had made the decision to try and break into Warren's house.

In retrospect, she shouldn't have done this.

A concerned neighbor had seen her skulking around the house, trying various doors and windows and had called the police. In short order, she'd found herself arrested for attempted breaking and entering and, while this could have been neatly avoided if Warren had returned home as scheduled, unfortunately he hadn't. His flight had been delayed. Unwilling to share her humiliation with anyone else, she'd used her one phone call and left the embarrassing can-you-please-come-bail-me-out-of-jail? request on his cell.

He had. He'd also broken up with her.

Julia sighed. The fact that she hadn't cried told her everything she needed to know about the state of her heart and the fact that he hadn't owned it. Was she disappointed that another relationship had come to an end? Yes. That was more disheartening than anything else. It felt like a personal failure on her part and it was especially infuriating when she, the so-called relationship expert, couldn't hold a man's interest for more than nine months at a time.

For whatever reason, nine months seemed to ring the death knell. The first three would pass in a romantic haze of new love, the next three would segue into a predictable sort of comfort, then by the ninth month, everything would have fallen apart.

On the two-hour drive down here this morning, Julia had systematically reviewed her last three break-ups and come to the unhappy conclusion that her poor performance in the bedroom was the problem. Clearly she was doing something wrong. To her own credit, however, the same men who complained about her being uptight had never came away from her bed less than satisfied. She grimaced.

That role had been exclusively hers.

In fact, to be perfectly honest, if anyone had a right to complain it was *her*. She was the one who'd been cheated out of a sexually induced orgasm *every single time*.

Julia released a small breath. Unfortunately she couldn't deny the evidence and the evidence suggested that she was the one at fault. Given that, she'd come to the practical decision that some sexual instruction was in order. The minute she finished up this week-long workshop with Lieutenant Wicked, she fully intended to hook up with one of those guys she'd always avoided like the plague.

Guys like *him*.

Desperate? Insane? Yes on both counts, but she was tired of always coming up short—literally—and the only way she could logically imagine remedying the situation was by learning from an expert. That's why aspiring artists studied the masters, she told herself, why students learned from their professors.

And as galling as it was to admit it, she needed a player—a guy who was only interested in a brief encounter punctuated with lots of hot sex. A serial sex artist, someone who specialized in catch and release.

An image of Guy McCann leapt instantly to mind, making her fingers tighten around the steering wheel and her breath thin in her lungs.

No doubt he'd do nicely, she thought, then immediately tamped down that line of thinking. Aside from the fact that she was here in a business capacity—representing her father, no less—Julia had the sneaking suspicion that Guy McCann would be hard to… manage.

Her gaze darted to her rearview mirror once more. Designer shades covered his eyes and he drove with one hand on the wheel, the other slung carelessly across the back of the seat. Windows open, the breeze ruffled his black locks adding more irreverent charisma to his already considerable charm.

No doubt about it, Julia thought as a hot tingle pinged her sex, he had the wow factor in spades.

And every other trump card, as well.

Julia paused consideringly. No, she decided. *No.*

It was out of the question. Aside from deciding to instantly dislike him on a personal level, if Julia had learned one thing in the course of her career it was how to spot a guy with *issues*.

And from the guarded look she'd glimpsed in those admittedly beautiful eyes, to the uncompromising set of his shoulders, it was clear that Guy McCann's issues had issues. Furthermore, though she'd been being a smart-ass—albeit an insightful one—when she'd pointed out that Garrett had put a guy he didn't trust in charge of a trust-building course, she seriously had to wonder about that. She didn't know what Garrett's game was, but clearly there was more at work here than what she realized.

At any rate, though her first instinct was to help—to jump right in and "meddle" as her father had always said—she didn't want any part of it. She'd come to Fort Benning to do a job—to pay back an old debt—and she would do that to the best of her ability. Colonel Garrett had saved her father's life. The least she could do was remain a professional and complete the favor he'd asked of her.

As for Guy McCann…he'd successfully paddled his own canoe for thirty-odd years. He could certainly manage without what she instinctively knew he'd deem as interference.

Five minutes later, Julia angled her car into a space near Olson Hall, grabbed her purse and made for the sidewalk. Though it was early spring, she could feel the promise of heat and humidity in the air and the smell of fresh-cut grass tickled her nose. Spring was her favorite season, when bugs were at a minimum and everything became new again. There was something about the symbolism of rebirth associated with the season that really appealed to her. For whatever reason, she longed for her own rebirth. Her skin felt too tight for her body and there was a sense of urgency—of desperation—that hovered around her shoulders like a shadow she couldn't shake.

And speaking of shadows... She felt Guy McCann fall in behind her, his tall frame looming over her. Her stomach did an odd little flutter and the palms of her hands tingled, forcing her to set her jaw against the unfamiliar sensation.

"Are we racing?" he drawled, his smooth voice laced with humor.

"No," Julia replied tightly.

He hummed under his breath, hurried forward when she reached the door so that he could open it for her. "I wondered. You kept picking up speed."

"That's because I was trying to get away from you."

He feigned a wince. "Ouch."

Julia shot him a look over her shoulder as she entered the air-conditioned lobby. "Oh, please." She'd bet a bayonet couldn't puncture that ego.

"There's no point in trying to avoid me," Guy told her, seemingly unoffended. "Have you forgotten about dinner?"

As if. "I suspect I won't be hungry."

Julia presented her ID to the clerk and waited to be checked into a room, determinedly looking at anything but him.

Unfortunately that didn't prevent her from *feeling* him. It was as though he emanated a magnetic charge, flooding the air with his very presence and for whatever reason, she seemed particularly susceptible to it. She'd never been so…*aware* of another person.

"Hungry or not, we're supposed to get acquainted. We're going to be working together, after all."

There was that, Julia knew. Still, the idea of

spending any time alone with him made her nervous. Possibly because she didn't trust herself not to take advantage of him. The idea drew a smile. *Her* take advantage of *him?* No doubt that thought would put a smile on his provokingly handsome face, Julia thought, wondering about his sudden desire to make nice. She mentally harrumphed.

He certainly hadn't been interested in being nice to her a few minutes ago. Hell, he hadn't so much as looked at her until she'd sat down next to him, and even then his first look hadn't been at her face, which would have been re-spectful—instead she'd caught him checking out her leg.

Gratifying, she had to admit.

She'd felt the weight of that hot stare as though he'd touched her. Felt it sizzle a path up her leg, over her breast and then ultimately settle on her face. At that point she'd been so mesmer-ized over his she hadn't had the presence of mind to gauge his reaction to hers, but Julia knew most men found her passably attractive.

Her nose was too big—had been the bane of her existence for as long as she could remember—but the idea of changing it had always been out of the question. She'd grown too used to seeing it in the middle of her face to muck around with things. Imperfections added character, in her opinion, and so long as her nose functioned properly she'd leave it alone.

Truthfully, she suspected it bothered her mother more than it did herself. Her mother had petitioned for rhinoplasty many times over the years, always calling it "that unfortunate nose." She'd even gone so far as to make Julia an appointment with her own personal plastic surgeon, but Julia had refused to go.

Having become the Plastic Surgery Queen, her mother's face had been stretched and injected with Botox until she looked more like a wax figure than a person. Her most recent procedure had been a hand lift. Julia's lips quirked. Why not? she thought. Everything else had been lifted, tucked, plucked and tattooed to perfection.

As an adult it was easy to see that her mother's self-worth was hopelessly entangled with her beauty, but as a child, then an insecure teenager, being under constant scrutiny and criticism hadn't been easy. She'd once overheard her parent's arguing about it.

*"We've got to do something about that nose, Frank,"* her mother had said, disgusted. *"It's horrid."*

*"It's not horrid, Joan,"* came her father's long-suffering reply. *"Our daughter is beautiful. Leave her alone. You're going to give her a complex."*

*Too late,* Julia had thought.

*"But don't you think if—"*

*"Enough!"* her father had finally snapped. *"She's not you, dammit. She doesn't have to be perfect. Just leave her alone."*

She hadn't, of course, but knowing that her father thought she was beautiful had warmed her heart and instantly perked up her flagging self-esteem. It had been equally validating and liberating and, while her mother's criticism could usually find a mark, after that moment, it hadn't hurt as much as before. She'd been inoculated, for lack of a better explanation.

Julia accepted her key and listened while the clerk told her where to find her lodgings. Rather than staying there, she'd been booked into a nearby duplex. "It has a kitchen and a nice front porch," the clerk told her. "You'll like it."

Julia smiled her thanks and turned to go.

"And, of course former Lieutenant Colonel McCann will be your neighbor."

She paused, her grin frozen. "How nice," Julia murmured. Actually, it was the polar opposite of nice. A helpless cloak of doom settled around her shoulders and she briefly entertained asking for a room here instead.

On the smug scale, Guy's smile would have registered an easy ten. "Isn't it, though?"

Geez Lord, he was infuriating, Julia thought, wondering why she also found that completely irresistible. No doubt the trip to the slammer last night had damaged her psyche. Something had happened to her, otherwise she wouldn't be torn between the pressing urge to slap him or kiss him. Actually, slapping him, then kissing him, then slapping him again vastly appealed to her. The idea drew a smile.

"What time would you like to get together for dinner?" Guy asked, accepting his own key.

Julia rolled her eyes. "Never-thirty."

He looked away, seemingly torn between laughing and throttling her. "Six it is, then."

"But—"

He flashed another cocky grin at her, but this one held a bit of an edge which, to her eternal stupidity, she found secretly thrilling. "I'll knock."

*Six*, Julia thought, releasing a resigned breath. *Her date with doom.*

And yet she looked forward to it. How screwed up was that?

# 3

GUY PEERED BEHIND THE curtain of his living-room window and watched as Julia unloaded a couple of grocery bags from the back seat of her car. Using her trusty map of the base, she'd unerringly found her way to their duplex, then wheeled her rolling bag up the sidewalk and into the house.

Fifteen minutes later—just time enough for her to unpack, he suspected—he'd heard her door close as she'd exited the house once more, and when he'd appeared on his own porch and casually asked where she was off to, she'd shot him a long-suffering look and told him that she wanted a few things from the grocery store.

In other words, she might have to share a

meal with him tonight, but the rest of the week she'd eat in.

Excellent, Guy thought. She could cook for him.

The thought made him chuckle. In all seriousness, with the exception of Payne, he didn't think he'd ever seen a more efficient person. He'd bet his right nut that she was a list maker, too, one of those people who had to write things down to keep track, then felt a satisfying sense of accomplishment the minute she checked another item off her to-do list.

The laptop case he'd noted suggested she appreciated technology, but the beat-up attaché told him that she had an admirable sentimental streak. Given that, he imagined that a plain old pad of notebook paper held her lists and not a trendy PDA. For whatever reason, the idea brought another unexpected smile to his lips.

Odd, when less than an hour ago he'd been mad enough to spit nails. At Garrett, he'd realized, not her, which was why he'd felt like a sanctimonious bastard for hurting her feelings. That one unguarded look she'd flashed him when he'd suggested she was a tight ass was enough to make him feel like a first class SOB and, while he hadn't been backpedaling, per se, or had a change of heart about working with her—he still didn't like it—he couldn't very well take out Garrett's duplicity on her. This was between him and the Colonel and unfortunately she'd been caught in the cross fire.

Hurting her feelings had been small and mean and, unaccustomed to feeling regret when it came to a female, it had taken Guy a few seconds to realize that was exactly what had made him so damned uncomfortable on the drive over to Olson Hall.

Furthermore, she intrigued the hell out of him.

Guy had been around enough women to know the usual score. No brag just fact, but he had good instincts, had always relied on them and he'd always been particularly good at sizing a person up. He could spot a needy chick at twenty paces, a liar in fifty. He could tell who was jonesing for revenge sex, who was simply horny and who was looking for a husband. He'd never met a woman he couldn't read, couldn't gauge in an instant…and yet he couldn't get a firm line on Julia Beckam.

She was so damned proper looking he wanted to shake her and, though it could only be wishful thinking on his part, he got the distinct impression that she wanted someone to rock her world. That she was waiting for it. Odd, he knew, when she looked wound tighter than an eight-day clock. That bun she'd screwed that beautiful hair into worked his last nerve. Didn't she know it only made a guy want to take it down and mess it up? His fingers practically itched to do just that.

Among other things.

His cell rang from the clip at his waist, snagging his attention, which was just as well because she'd mounted the steps to the porch and would be going in where he couldn't puzzle over her anymore.

At least, not until dinner.

"McCann," he said, his typical greeting.

"How's it going?" Payne asked.

Guy moved away from the window and dropped heavily into a recliner. "It blows." And that was putting it mildly.

Evidently realizing just that, Payne asked the right question. "Any surprises?"

"Julia Beckam," Guy drawled.

Silence, then, "Who is Julia Beckam?"

"That's exactly what I asked Garrett. She's a relationship therapist he's brought in as my co-instructor." He could hear the sarcasm in his own voice.

"He didn't tell you about her?"

Guy blew out a breath. "That's why it was a surprise."

"A relationship therapist for a special forces team?" Payne asked skeptically.

"Garrett wants these boys to feel married in all but the biblical sense," Guy said. "And this is not just any special forces team. It's Project Chameleon's replacement."

"You're shittin' me."

He wished, Guy thought. Logic told him that the army would have immediately wanted to reassemble a replacement unit to supplant theirs, but the idea of another group of men assuming Project Chameleon was somehow disheartening. Ego, most likely. Hell, guys like him didn't sign up to do the hard work without the necessary ego to back it up. He smiled. It was part of their charm. Or so he'd been told.

While he admittedly missed parts of the old lifestyle, Guy knew he didn't have any desire to go back to work for Uncle Sam. Simply being back on base made him feel like he was smothering in regret and failure. Dealing with Danny's death was painful enough, but for reasons which escaped him, being here—in this place—made it worse. Too many good memories mixed in with the bad, he supposed.

Furthermore, while he was thankful to the army for everything he'd learned—the discipline, values and education—he'd adjusted to civilian life without incident. He was close enough to Alabama to visit his mother when he wanted, but far enough away that she wouldn't cling. As for his father—instant hatred welled inside him—Guy didn't give a damn if he ever saw that sorry sack of shit ever again. He could rot in hell and the sooner the better, as far as Guy was concerned.

Hard? Maybe so. But not as hard as his father used to hit him.

Respect was earned—not a parental right—and his old man would never have his.

"Want me to come over there and help you?" Payne asked. "Jamie's here for the moment. I could get away for a few days."

The offer was nothing less than what he would expect from his friend, but Guy found himself uncharacteristically touched all the same. Payne and Jamie were like the brothers he'd never had, his adopted family. Danny had been, too, which had made Guy's ultimate betrayal all the more difficult. Being responsible for any death was a blow, but that of a friend, of a person you loved and had loved you…

Guy cleared his throat. "No, but thanks."

"Is there anything I can do here on this end?"

Actually… "Run a background check on Julia Beckam," Guy said, thinking about that enigmatic "unavoidably detained" comment she'd made this morning. Forewarned was forearmed and he wanted to know exactly who he was dealing with before they went to dinner. "If you can get back with me before six that would be great."

"Will do," Payne told him. "What about Garrett? Have you discovered his angle yet?"

Garrett hadn't cashed in a single favor where it hadn't directly benefited him, so there was no reason to suspect that he'd change the status quo with Guy. On the surface, asking him to come in and teach a trust-building class for a special forces team seemed harmless, but they'd all learned the hard way that Garrett didn't do anything without motive. He definitely had something to gain by ensuring Guy's participation. The million-dollar question of course was: what?

"Not yet," Guy finally told him. "I'm gonna do a little digging around here and see what the rumor mill is churning."

"Shit, most likely," Payne said, chuckling.

Guy laughed, conceding the point. "So long as nothing's changed."

"Listen," Payne said, hesitating enough to indicate a subject change. "I need to make sure that you're going to be back here on Saturday."

"Sure," Guy said, puzzled by the remark and slight…nervousness he detected in his friend's voice. Payne? Nervous? He frowned. "My last class is over at noon on Friday, so I should be home that night. Why?"

"I'm getting married Saturday." Matter of fact, in typical Payne form, as though he hadn't just announced something huge.

Particularly considering that Payne swore to never marry.

His parents had set a lousy example for the institution and his father had routinely been swindled out of millions of Payne's ultimate inheritance by greedy women.

Guy knew that Payne had proposed to Emma and he also knew that Payne was never a man to go back on his word. When it came to moral fiber, The Specialist had it in spades. He wouldn't have proposed to Emma had he not wanted to marry her, but Payne was a methodical planner by nature and if he'd had anything in the works, Guy had certainly not heard anything about it.

"I knew you were getting married, but I didn't realize you'd set a date yet."

"It was a spur of the moment decision."

Payne? Spur of the moment? A sneaking suspicion began to form. "Has something happened to hasten your plans?" Guy asked suspiciously.

"She's not pregnant," Payne told him, following Guy's line of thinking. "Though I'd be thrilled if she was."

"Then what's the hurry? I thought you wanted to wait until summer. You know, while she was on summer vacation." She'd enrolled in vet school shortly after moving to Atlanta with Payne.

"That was the original plan and she has no idea that it's changed, so just show up and keep your mouth shut when you get here."

Guy felt his eyes bug. *"You mean she doesn't know you're getting married on Saturday?"* he asked, astounded. "Don't you think you'd better check with her first?" He leaned forward in his chair. "Isn't that something the *bride* should be aware of?"

"It's a surprise, smart-ass. I've booked The Atrium and I've talked to her mother. She came into town a few days ago and she and Emma went shopping for her gown under the pretense of 'being prepared.' It's all arranged."

It certainly sounded like it. What other people spent more than a year planning, he'd pulled together in less than a week. Just another example of money talks. God only knows what Payne had forked over to make this wedding happen this quickly. What the hell had happened? Guy wondered. What had prompted him to deviate from "the plan" and tie the knot now?

"It's killing you, isn't it?" Payne asked, laughing softly and seemingly pleased with himself.

"It's out of character, that's for damned sure. And yes, dammit," he admitted, exasperated. "I'm curious. What happened? Why now?"

"You won't understand."

"Try me."

He hesitated for a moment. "A couple of nights ago, we were sitting on the couch watching TV—something pointless but entertaining—and she was curled up next to me, her hand in mine and…" He laughed softly. "And I looked down and thought, what the hell am I waiting for? I love this woman. I saw our future and that was that. Honestly, Guy, I proposed because I was afraid of losing her. I wanted to marry her, of course—I wouldn't have asked otherwise—but…" He let go a breath. "I'm not afraid anymore, if that makes sense."

Naturally he couldn't relate, but it did make sense. "Of course," Guy said. "Congratulations, man. I'm happy for you." A thought struck. "What about a tux?" Payne owned one, but he and Jamie had never had the need.

"No worries. I took some things from your closet for measurements. It might not be the best fit, but nobody's gonna be looking at you anyway."

Guy laughed. "Bastard."

"Maybe. But I'm a happy bastard."

"Call me when you get that info on Julia, will you?"

"I will. Julia," he repeated consideringly. "It's an old-fashioned name."

Fishing and not too subtly, Guy thought, mildly exasperated. He knew where this was going and he didn't like it one damned bit. "She's not old." He'd find out soon enough, anyway when he ran the background check. There was no point in lying.

Payne hummed under his breath. "Pretty?"

"You could say that." He could, too, but wasn't going to be baited into it. Besides, pretty didn't begin to cover it. She was breathtaking.

"Should we worry?"

"Worry about your wedding. I'm good here."

"I'll be in touch," Payne told him.

He was counting on it, Guy thought. He didn't know what he expected Payne to find on Julia but the tingling in his gut—one he knew better than to ignore—told him he was onto something. Hell, everyone had secrets. A smile caught the corner of his mouth.

Some were just more interesting than others.

JULIA STOOD IN THE LIVING ROOM of her duplex, looked around in a vain attempt to find something else to do, but ultimately conceded defeat. Her cheeks puffed as she exhaled heavily and she settled herself on one end of the couch, tucking her feet up under her. She was at a loss and knew where her mind would take her if she let it run amok. Instead she reviewed her progress.

She'd unpacked, been to the grocery store and stocked up on a few things, the most important of which was tea. She preferred hot tea in the mornings as opposed to coffee and was secretly pleased that she'd have a kitchen. She'd never bought into the whole what's-the-point-of-cooking-for-one mentality. She loved good food and she loved to cook. Eating alone was hard enough, without throwing a generic frozen dinner into the mix. A smile quirked her lips. She'd have grilled salmon with mango chutney and a nice white wine, thank you very much. If she was going to eat alone, she might as well enjoy it.

Furthermore, cooking would guarantee no more dinner rendezvous with Guy. She'd never been a girl scout, but that hadn't prevented her from learning how to be prepared.

The duplex was lovely, an old two-story house which had been divided for the sake of efficiency. A large eat-in kitchen, living room and a half bath downstairs, two bedrooms and full bath up. Beat-up hardwood floors and tall ceilings added character and a host of mismatched furniture provided extra charm. It was cozy, Julia decided, and much preferred to a sterile hotel room.

In many ways it reminded her of home. She'd bought a little craftsmen fixer-upper just outside of Atlanta three years ago and had been painstakingly restoring things a room at a time. She was a room away from being finished—a guest bedroom—and then she planned to start working more on the landscaping.

Presently she kept a small herb garden with only tomatoes and peppers, but she longed for more room and more vegetables. Actually, she wanted to plant a few rows of corn, but couldn't see her neighbors appreciating that.

Wow, Julia thought, marveling at her train of thought. It looked like she was prepared to go to extreme lengths to avoid thinking about Guy McCann being right next door. Even this was a new one for her—hot guy or planting corn?

Sheesh, she thought with a silent whimper. She was in trouble.

She'd hurried around getting everything in order—her fix for stress—and the whole time she'd been annoyingly aware of the fact that only a wall separated them, when it didn't seem potent enough to stop his appeal. In less than fifteen minutes he'd knock at her door and collect her for dinner, the one Garrett had suggested, so she couldn't very well refuse.

In truth, Julia realized that their meeting before their classes started in the morning was a good idea. Professional and all that. But keeping it professional with a guy like him… Well, that was going to be the true test of her character and, considering she desperately needed to rip a seam in her moral fiber to fix her sexual performance—and he was exactly the type of guy she needed to do it for her—she knew she was wading into uncharted waters.

Hot water, no doubt, she thought, if that incinerating stare she'd felt as she'd walked up the sidewalk a little while ago was any indication.

She didn't have to look up to know that he'd been standing at the window watching her. Just like before, she could *feel* it. Not the typical someone's-looking-at-me sensation, either. This was more potent. Lethal. It made her spine tingle, her breasts quicken and her belly inflate with fizzy air.

Quite honestly, she didn't think she'd ever been around a man who affected her more. She wanted to chalk it up to her recent plan to find a sexual instructor, but instinctively knew that wasn't the case.

Guy McCann elicited strong emotions from her and thus far they'd run the gamut of wanting to slap his smug face to wanting to kiss the irreverent smile right off his lips. Un-accustomed to not being in complete control of her emotions, Julia knew her ability to reason had been severely compromised as well, otherwise she wouldn't be fantasizing about making Guy her sex tutor.

It was out of the question, she told herself. Ludicrous. She was here in a professional capacity for chrissakes, representing her father. To use this convenient opportunity away from home for her own personal gain had to be wrong. Sure, it wasn't like they'd be doing it in the classroom in front of their pupils, but still…

If she took advantage of him, it would be after she'd already conducted her lesson for the day, when her time was her own, but—

A knock sounded at her front door, preventing her from completing the thought. Julia's gaze darted to her watch and she tamped down a surge of irritation, then got up and opened the door.

Looking freshly showered, devastatingly sexy and a little too confident and amused for her comfort, Guy stood on her front porch. "You're early," Julia said by way of greeting.

Guy consulted his cell phone for the time and frowned. "Sorry. Do you want me to come back in three minutes?"

"No," she said. He kept glancing from her to his cell phone and back as though doing some sort of comparison. Julia paused. "Is something wrong?"

"No, no," Guy said, scrutinizing the image on his cell phone again. He held it up for her inspection and the picture she saw there made her belly tip in a nauseated roll.

*Her mug shot.*

How in God's name had he—

"Personally, I think you should have just left your hair down instead of using the wig, but I have to admit it's pretty damned sexy." He flashed a grin that would have made a rose bloom in the artic circle and a hopeful furrow emerged between his brows. "You didn't happen to bring that dress, did you?"

# 4

THEY SAY A PICTURE IS worth a thousand words, but Guy would have to deem this particular photo priceless. He grinned.

Because it matched the look on her face.

Julia gaped, eyes wide, and high color rose in her cheeks. "Where did you get that?" she demanded, albeit weakly.

He snapped his phone shut. "A friend. I'm famished," he said, retracing his steps off her porch. He looked around and took a deep cleansing breath, as though all was right with his world. "Are you hungry?"

She hurriedly locked her door, then scrambled along behind him. He decided he liked it, her chasing after him for a change. *Go ahead*, he thought. *Check out my ass. I happen to like it.*

"What friend?" she wanted to know.

Guy chuckled under his breath and opened the passenger door for her. "Boy when you said 'unavoidably detained' you meant it, didn't you? The guy who bailed you out of jail, this Warren, is he your boyfriend?"

Surely not, Guy had thought skeptically when he'd first seen his picture, as well. Bless Payne's thorough heart, he'd run a check on him, too. The guy looked about as fun as watching paint dry, downright maudlin. He'd dubbed him Eeyore, and one look at him had told him that the guy didn't possess the necessary skill to rock her world.

Her?

With him?

What? Did she have a "boring" fetish?

Unfortunately, since it was his house she'd been arrested for attempted B & E—dressed up like a comic-book bombshell, no less—and he'd been the guy she'd called to the rescue, Guy had come to unhappy conclusion that Eeyore had to be her boyfriend.

It boggled the mind.

Though he knew he shouldn't give a damn, the mere idea set his teeth on edge. He—a badass former Ranger—was jealous of a man with absolutely no discernible evidence of testosterone. A bloody tax accountant.

"How do you know about Warren?" she asked as Guy slid behind the wheel. He started the truck, then dialed the stereo down to accommodate conversation.

"He bailed you out," Guy said. He shifted into drive, shot a look over his shoulder, then pulled away from the curb. "You were trying to break into his house. My friend thought I'd want to know these things."

Her jaw worked angrily. "Did it ever occur to your friend that none of this is any of your business?" she practically ground out.

Guy flashed her an unrepentant smile and dropped his shades into place. "No."

*"No?"*

"Why would it? We're in the business of not minding our business."

She frowned. "Come again?"

"Ranger Security," Guy told her. He aimed his truck toward Frank's, a nice little Italian place off base. "A couple of friends and I run a personal security and P.I. firm in Atlanta. We earn our living by being nosy, though personally, I prefer the term 'curious.'"

She snorted. "Call it whatever you want it, but you had no business delving into my private life. What on earth would make you want to do a thing like that?" she asked, a mortified wail creeping into her voice.

Guy slid her a lingering look and lowered his voice an octave. "I was curious."

Julia blushed adorably and looked away. "You could have just asked."

"But then I wouldn't have this hot new screen saver for my cell phone."

A smile played around her lips before she could fully squash it. "You're insufferable."

Guy shrugged. "I've been called worse."

"I'll just bet you have."

"So what's the deal with Eeyore, I mean Warren?" Guy asked again. "You never answered me."

She turned to look at him. "Eeyore?" she asked pointedly.

He slid her a sidelong glance. "Surely you've seen the resemblance."

Julia chuckled and shook her head, evidently not quite sure what to make of him. "You're a piece of work, you know that?"

"And you're really good at avoiding questions. Maybe I should call my friend back and have him get the score from Warren. You know, it's amazing how people will just spill their guts to you. Really. You wouldn't believe some of the—"

She gasped, looking distinctly uncomfortable. "You wouldn't."

He tutted under his breath and smiled innocently at her. "Aw, you ought to know me better than that."

Looking completely irritated and miserable, Julia crossed her arms over her chest and stared out the windshield. "He *was* my boy-friend," she finally said. "We broke up."

Before or after he'd bailed her out of jail? Guy wondered, curiously elated at this news. It meant that she was unattached and available and though he shouldn't be considering any sort of sexual entanglement with her, he had to admit the idea was becoming more and more seductive.

Had she dressed up for Warren as a way to win him back? Geez God, surely not. Where was her self-esteem? Her self-respect? Or had Eeyore dumped her after her untimely stint in the slammer? For whatever reason, this seemed more likely. She hadn't cut him loose, that was for sure, otherwise she wouldn't have been planning a sexy little rendezvous featuring her in the starring role.

As unbelievable as it was, Eeyore had dumped *her*.

He smothered a disbelieving grunt. Boring *and* stupid. Now there was a winning combination. What the hell had she been thinking?

Granted he'd known her less than a day, but even he could see that this Warren hadn't been the guy for her. He'd had *chesticles* for pity's sake, big man boobs. Hell, the guy probably had more estrogen than she did.

Since she seemed more humiliated than hurt, Guy decided to continue his roll as nosy ass and probe for further details. "Why'd you break up?"

Her lips formed a humorless smile. "Like a dog with a bone, aren't you? I'll bet you were one of those kids who liked poking dead animals with sticks to see if they were really dead."

"No, I wasn't," Guy said, stung. He loved animals, dammit, and while he'd admit to being a hellion, he'd never been a bully. Or a psychopath in the making. He shot her a glance. "My dog would take offense at the comment."

"You've got a dog?"

Her brows winged up in surprise, as though he were too shallow to care for a pet. Guy set his jaw and found himself becoming more and more perturbed. "Yes," he said tightly. "I have a dog—Bear. He's a chocolate lab."

"Oh."

He waited a beat and when she didn't expand on comment he said, "Why would you think I wouldn't have a dog?"

"I just assumed you wouldn't have time for one," she said breezily. "An animal requires a commitment and, what with all your snooping around and womanizing, I wouldn't have figured you'd invest that much of yourself into a pet."

"And I wouldn't have thought you'd dress up like a hooker to try and drum up some sexual interest in your boring boyfriend, then get yourself thrown into the slammer for your trouble, either." He smiled wolfishly at her. "But I guess we all make mistakes."

Back to being mean again and he instantly regretted it, but dear God, the woman was provoking.

"I'm sorry," Guy told her, mentally swearing. "That was uncalled for."

Julia sighed heavily. "Don't apologize. I goaded you."

"That's no excuse for being cruel. You just—" Guy paused, trying to think of a diplomatic way to say what he meant, which was highly unusual for him when he normally didn't use an internal editor.

"Don't sugarcoat it," she told him, smiling now. "Just say what you mean. First lesson in building a trusting relationship, right?"

"Fine." He glared at her with exasperated humor. "You annoy the shit out of me." He grunted, drummed his fingers against the steering wheel. "You're such a smart-ass."

She rolled her eyes. "Hi, Pot. Meet Kettle."

"I know I'm a smart-ass," Guy readily admitted. "I'm just not used to dealing with a woman who's one also." Actually, it was kind of refreshing. Women didn't ordinarily argue with him. They batted their lashes and sat in his lap and ruffled his hair. Conversation was limited.

She smiled and chewed the inside of her cheek. "No, you're probably used to women fawning all over you and agreeing with every macho prehistoric comment that comes out of that sexy mouth of yours."

He brightened. "You think my mouth is sexy?"

Julia closed her eyes tightly shut, then opened them again and chuckled softly. "Out of everything I said *that's* the only thing you heard?"

Guy wheeled his truck into Frank's parking lot and found an empty space. "No, I heard the rest of it. I just liked that part the best."

She blushed again, fought another smile. "You would."

"Hey, if it makes you feel any better, I think your mouth is sexy, too." Without thinking, he reached over, cupped her chin and gently ran the pad of his thumb over her bottom lip. She gasped softly, the sound vibrating something deep inside of him, and those mesmerizing green eyes fluttered shut.

Invitation enough, Guy thought, closing the distance between them.

His mouth settled over hers and a shock of sensation so intense it made every hair on his body stand on end—along with another part below his waist—shook him to the very core. His entire body quaked with a weird sensation akin to adrenaline overload—as a junkie, he recognized it—and a shaky breath leaked out of his mouth and into hers. She tasted like sweet tea and butterscotch candy and the vaguest hint of something wild, wicked and indefinable.

He became instantly addicted.

She hesitated for a fraction of a second, then she sighed—the sweetest breath of supplication he'd ever tasted—pushed her hands into his hair and her tongue into his mouth and the rest of the world vanished.

He'd been right.

She was a hellion in the making—and he was just the guy to help her with the transformation.

IT WAS OFFICIAL, Julia decided.

She was a slut.

She'd known Guy McCann for less than day and yet the second he'd touched her—just the barest graze of the pad of his thumb across her bottom lip, probably the single most erotic touch she'd ever been privy to—and she'd *melted*.

Right into his mouth.

Truthfully, she hadn't expected him to kiss her—a pretty bold move for a guy who'd she'd spent the majority of the time arguing with—but then who was she kidding? She'd known from the minute she'd met him that he played by his own rules. He was cocky, reckless and irreverent, infuriating…and absolutely sexy as hell.

*And, oh Lord, he could kiss like the very devil.*

He fed at her mouth with a combination of confidence and skill that was simply drugging with its sensuality. A bold sweep of his tongue, the smooth drag of his lips over hers. He'd leaned over and had framed both hands around her face, angling her closer so that he could deepen the kiss. She felt his fingers slid over her jaw, almost reverently, and a satisfied masculine growl of approval vibrated in their joined mouths.

Julia's belly quivered, her nipples pearled

and an explosion of heat erupted in her womb, sending a rush of warmth over the quaking, tingling folds of her sex.

*Sweet mercy.*

She tangled her fingers in the short hair at his nape, sliding her thumb along the smooth patch of skin behind his ear and wiggled closer to him. Her blood burned through her veins, moving sluggishly with the weight of desire, and seemed to burn hotter in her suddenly heavy breasts and needy, neglected womb.

A kiss, a mere kiss, and yet if he so much as touched her, she knew she'd come.

*This* was what she'd been missing, Julia realized as a buzz of excitement joined the tornado of sensation swirling madly through her body.

*This* was pure desire in its most potent form.

Mindless. Desperate. Agonizingly unfamiliar because she'd never experienced anything even remotely close to this sort of passion. Every cell in her body hammered with the urge to get closer, to feel naked skin to naked skin, his mouth attached to her nipple, the hard long thrust of him deep inside of her.

She whimpered longingly into his mouth and felt him smile against her lips, then seemingly pleased and further emboldened, he upped the tempo of the kiss. Suckling her tongue, probing the insides of her mouth, and all the while, moving those amazing lips over hers in a mimicking dance she'd love to feel below her waist. If he could make this kind of magic in her mouth, then the possibilities were endless on other equally sensitive body parts.

To her chagrin, Guy drew back. Her swollen lips and drunken expression peered back at her from his mirrored shades. A slow smile slid across his lips. "Thank you."

"For what?" she asked stupidly.

"For not slapping me. I've been wanting to do that since the instant I saw your mouth."

She blinked. The instant he saw her mouth? But—

"It's hot. And you're a helluva kisser. Good timing. Not too wet, not too dry. *Wow.*"

Spoken like a true teacher, Julia thought, still swaddled in the post-kiss afterglow. And he'd complimented her. Now that was a first.

Guy shot her another smile, then exited the truck, rounded the hood and opened her door for her. Good manners, she thought, wondering where he'd learned them. His mother, most likely, yet it was hard to imagine this man ever being a baby or even a little boy. Her lips twisted. He could hardly spring fully grown from the womb, though, so she knew he had to have been, at one time or another, a least a little vulnerable.

He fell in beside her as they walked toward the restaurant. "I hope you like Italian," he said, holding the door open for her.

The mouthwatering scent of fresh garlic, oil olive and marinara hung in the air, making her belly rumble. Candle light sparkled from small square tables draped in red-and-white checked clothes. "You wouldn't have to hope if you'd asked," she pointed out, trying to appear less affected than she had been by that kiss.

Guy smiled, completely unrepentant. "Is that your way of telling me that you *don't* like it?"

They waited to be seated. "No, that's my way of telling you that you should have asked me where I would like to go."

"I wasn't aware that this was a date."

Julia chewed the inside of her cheek and glared at him. "I wasn't either until you kissed me."

He grinned and an admiring gleam twinkled in that smooth jade gaze. "Touché. Do you like Italian?" he asked solicitously.

Julia nodded primly. "As it happens, I do."

He put a knuckle in the small of her back, causing a ripple of gooseflesh to zip up her spine, and nudged her forward, after the hostess. "Excellent. Then I made a wise choice."

Despite it being high-handed, yes he had, Julia thought as they were seated. Fresh herbs, oil and bread appeared at their table almost instantly, followed by a nice bottle of wine. The atmosphere was warm and casual and the aroma of good authentic Italian food wafted on the breeze of slowly turning ceiling fans. Julia ordered the spinach ravioli and a Caesar salad, then sat back and watched Guy peruse the menu with a practiced eye.

God, the man was too handsome for words, she thought, her gaze inexplicably drawn to those beautiful lips she'd been tasting only moments ago. "I'll have the grilled lamb with salsa verde," he said, closing his menu. "And a Caesar salad, also." Smiling, his gaze returned to Julia as soon as the waitress moved away. "So, why did you and Warren break up?"

Because I suck in the sack, Julia thought, and almost blurted out the humiliating truth. Her wine glass paused halfway at her lips and she looked at Guy above the rim. Tension knotted her belly. "Back to that, are we?"

"You've never answered me."

She swallowed. "That's because it's none of your business."

He tore off a piece of bread and dredged it in herbs and oil, then smiled at her before popping a bite into his mouth. "We're dating now, so it is."

She chuckled despite herself. "Oh, for Pete's sake, we aren't dating," Julia said, with an exasperated eye roll. "I was only needling you because you were rude. We kissed, Guy. That's it." She congratulated herself when no bolt of lightening accompanied the lie.

"For now," he murmured enigmatically, causing her heart to skip a beat. "If you aren't going to tell me why you two broke up, I suppose I'll simply have to start guessing." He paused, gave her a speculative look. "Despite the fact that you're incredibly beautiful, you're hiding a hideous deformity beneath that long skirt. Is that it?"

He was insane, Julia decided, warming at the "incredibly beautiful" remark. "No," she said, poking her tongue in her cheek.

"I'll look later," he said confidently.

Honestly, she'd like to get a look at his balls, because the guy had a brass set that was for damned sure.

He made a grand show of pondering her once more. "Any odd fetishes Lord Boring couldn't handle?" An exaggerated frown wrinkled his brow. "You're not into toe-sucking are you?"

She choked on a laugh. "No."

"Spanking?"

"No." Sorry. Pain in any shape, form or fashion didn't do it for her. She couldn't stub her toe without the entire neighborhood hearing her wail.

He hummed under his breath and leaned back in his chair, his expression turning endearingly dejected. "You aren't going to tell me, are you?"

"Why is it so important?"

"Because I find stupidity fascinating and the guy would have to be a complete moron to let you go."

Julia stilled, taken aback by the blunt but flattering assessment. That had to be one of the nicest things anyone had ever said to her. Her eyes inexplicably watered and she pretended to sneeze into her napkin so that she could wipe her eyes. "Thank you," she murmured. Then a thought struck. "What makes you so sure that he cut me loose and not the other way around?"

A droll smile rolled around his lips. "You weren't dressed like a woman who was going to give someone the kiss-off last night, were you?"

Oh, yeah. God, how humiliating. For a moment she'd actually forgotten that he'd stored that embarrassing mug shot on his cell phone, that he knew that she'd tried to break into Warren's house and that he'd been the one to bail her out of jail.

But if he knew all of that, he had to know that until last night she'd never been in any sort of trouble—that desperate times drove people to desperate measures. Hell, no wonder he was so damned curious. She'd be curious, too, if their roles were reversed.

In all honesty, she hadn't been desperate to keep Warren so much as she'd been desperate not to fail again. Which was hardly fair to

Warren. Still, the ungrateful wretch should have appreciated her gesture and not ditched her for her effort. Quite honestly, she never thought he would have had the spine to do it.

And *he had* been boring, Julia thought, growing more incensed by the second. He'd been a boring, snoring, soft-spoken mealy-mouthed stiff. What in the hell had she ever seen in him to start with? Julia wondered, delving into a little self-therapy. What had been the draw?

Then it hit her—he'd been safe and manageable…just like all the other guys she'd dated, Julia realized. Or since Colton, the one and only bad boy she'd ever allowed herself to care about. He'd dated her long enough to bed her—to make her think that he gave a damn about her—then had cut and run the minute he'd "tagged" her. He'd been her first. She'd been nineteen, a college freshmen, and fresh pickings for a guy whose only goal in life had been seeing how many girls he could assembly line through his bedroom.

God, that had been so long ago, Julia thought, still a bit stung by the rejection, but not devastated as she had been then. She stilled. Had she allowed that old heartbreak to affect all of her relationship decisions? Had the fear of being rejected again made her play it safe? To choose only guys she could conceivably control? She wouldn't have thought so, but… The subconscious was a powerful tool, and self-preservation even more so.

Her gaze slid to Guy once more. Now there was a heartbreaker if she'd ever seen one. Julia's breath left her in a soft sigh. He had trouble written all over him and yet that didn't prevent her pulse from leaping every time he aimed that smile at her. And he could fix her, Julia thought. That bone-melting kiss out in his truck had proved what she'd already suspected. When it came to the how-to's of sex, Guy McCann was clearly an expert.

She *needed* an expert.

She *needed* an orgasm.

In short, she needed him.

"Do you really want to know why he broke up with me?" she asked.

Guy nodded.

"Fine. I'll tell you." Julia tossed back the rest of her wine, drawing courage from the alcohol, then straightened her shoulders and pushed her lips into a bitter smile. "Lord Boring— *Eeyore*—thought I was too dull in the sack."

There. She'd either scared him off…or thrown down the gauntlet.

Time would only tell which.

# 5

GUY DIDN'T KNOW what he'd expected her to say, but that sure as hell wasn't it. Her? The little fire cracker he'd steamed up the windows of his truck with just a few minutes ago…too dull in the sack?

He instantly relived the feel of her tongue wrapping around his, her greedy hands kneading his scalp and shoulders, her pebbled breasts raking against his chest. Heat stirred in his loins, making his dick test the strength of his zipper.

*No fucking way.*

Either Eeyore had an off the charts kink factor—and given his hangdog expression, Guy found that very hard to believe—or he'd been too lazy a lover to satisfy Julia, then laid the blame at her door instead of claiming responsibility for his poor performance.

That seemed more likely. He snorted and shook his head. Selfish bastard.

Still… "Surely to God you don't believe that," Guy told her. She was a smart woman. She couldn't possibly believe that idiot, particularly given her response to him just a little while ago.

She shrugged, looking curiously resigned. "It's not the first time I've heard it."

"Then you're having sex with the wrong men. Trust me," he said, shooting her a smile. "You're hot."

Julia grinned, seemingly pleased, though a hint of skepticism still shadowed her gaze. "That's nice of you to say."

"I'm not just saying it, dammit. I know. I have carnal knowledge."

She chuckled, propped her chin in her palm and looked away. "You have *kissing* knowledge. There's a difference."

Tell that to his dick. Talk about *hard*

evidence. "Close enough," Guy said. "Eeyore's full of shit." He leaned back in his chair and laughed as a wonderful, purely selfish idea emerged. "I'd be willing to sleep with you to prove it," he offered magnanimously. He lifted his glass in her direction and broodingly considered her. "Just say the word and I'm there for you, baby."

Julia chewed the inside of her cheek and knowing humor danced in her pale green eyes. "I'll, uh… I'll be sure to keep that in mind."

"Seriously. It wouldn't be any trouble at all."

"I wouldn't want you to put yourself out," she said drolly.

His gaze tangled with hers. "I'm here to serve." Conversation paused as their salads arrived.

"You're supposed to be here for Colonel Garrett, not here to service me."

He pulled a negligent shrug, forked up a bite of lettuce drenched in dressing. "I'm open to perks."

Julia let go a shallow breath and for the

briefest moment he got the impression that she was actually considering it. First order of business, Guy thought—take down her hair. He didn't know how long it was, but given the size of the bun, he imagined that it would fall over her shoulders, possibly to her breasts. Ah…

*Rosy nipple, long blond curl…*

"Well, be that as it may, I'm here to repay a debt for my father." She grimaced. "Perks aren't included."

They'd get back to that later, Guy thought. In the mean time, he wanted to troll for some other information. "Garrett mentioned that you were the daughter of an old friend. What's the connection?" He doubted it had anything to do with his own favor, per se, but with the Colonel one never knew.

"My father and Colonel Garrett were in the same unit in Vietnam. My dad was wounded, would have died, but Garrett carried him to safety." She chewed the corner of her lip. "For obvious reasons, Dad was grateful. He left the military shortly after the war, but he and

Garrett have stayed in touch. They're both big Civil War buffs and belong to the same re-enactment group."

Guy inclined his head. He was fully aware of Garrett's Civil War obsession. He'd sent Payne to Gettysburg several months ago to retrieve a pocket watch which had been rumored to have belonged Robert E. Lee and lost during the Battle of Gettysburg. The damned thing had been undetected for almost one hundred and fifty years and yet Payne had found it within a week—on the chest of a cross-dressing potbellied pig, no less.

"Anyway, Colonel Garrett knew what I did for a living, that I have my own practice in Atlanta. I don't know whether my input for this training session was his brainchild—if he's pioneering it, so to speak—or if he'd gotten the idea from somewhere else, but he approached my father about it a little over two weeks ago." She scooted a crouton to the side of her plate with her fork. "Dad said he'd seemed a little…not desperate—" she winced as though not sure that was the right word "—but uncharacteristically anxious, at any rate, and he asked me if I could take this week off and help him out." She lifted a shoulder. "Knowing what he'd done for my Dad, how could I refuse?"

How indeed? And Guy would dearly love to know what had rattled the colonel's cage enough to make him anxious. Julia was right—that was severely out of character. And he'd be willing to bet his presence here was directly related to whatever had made the colonel uneasy.

Guy made a mental note to contact Payne when he got back to the house tonight. Instinct told him this was an important piece of information and though they'd been in the same unit, The Specialist had contacts still within the military that Guy didn't have access to. If he'd learned anything in this business, he'd learned that significant details could be found in the least likely of places and that Brian Payne was the best man at finding them.

"So why do you think Garrett enlisted your help?" Julia asked. "You're former military, right?"

Guy nodded, smiled as their entrees were delivered. "I'm a former unit leader," he told her, not altogether sure he wanted to have this conversation, but unable to see a way to avoid it. He carved off a bite of his lamb. "This team we're going to be working with is the replacement for the one me and my friends were a part of." He felt his lips twist and tried to keep the bitterness out of his voice. "According to Garrett he wants the 'benefit of my experience' imparted to these new guys."

"Have you had a chance to look over the curriculum Garrett gave us?"

He had. It contained the usual stuff—team-building exercises, critical-thinking skills, etcetera. Frankly, he wasn't altogether sure what Garrett hoped to accomplish by having him here. He didn't have anything new to impart. And the benefit of his experience? The only message he had for these guys was to expect the unexpected and know that no matter how thorough and foolproof your plan, your intel or your exit strategy, things could still go horribly, horribly wrong.

Danny's smiling face materialized in his mind's eye, causing his chest and throat to tighten. He set his loaded fork aside, unable to eat, and quaffed the rest of his wine.

Julia frowned. "Is something wrong with your meal?"

"No," Guy said, attempting to shake off the dread which had settled around his shoulders. "My eyes were just bigger than my stomach."

"Well, you've got to eat more than that, otherwise you're going to make me look like a hog. This is really good," she said, obviously enjoying her meal.

"I'm glad you like it."

A shadow fell over their table. "Well, I'll be damned," a familiar smart-assed voice said.

Guy felt every muscle in his body tense and he looked up.

*Richard Rutland.*

The bastard he, Jamie and Payne had thrashed the shit out of right after Danny had died. The jealous SOB had wanted Danny's spot on their team and had publicly gloated when Danny had been killed. He'd mouthed off about Danny "being stupid enough to get himself killed" and Jamie, who'd held Danny as he died and who'd carried his lifeless body back to their jeep, had roared in a rage of grief and tackled Rutland.

Honestly, they'd always hated Rutland and had secretly wanted to deck the bastard, so a part of Guy had been thrilled that he'd finally crossed a line and given him permission to do it. Even Payne, the most even tempered of all of them, had lost it that night.

"Guy?" Julia asked uncertainly as her wary gaze darted between the two of them.

Guy leveled a lethal stare at Rutland. "I'm sure you are," he said, referencing the asshole's I'll-be-damned comment.

Rutland rocked back on his heels and seemed secretly pleased, as though he was privy to some information that Guy didn't have. "Well, well, well. I wondered how he meant to play it. Gotta give Garrett his due. He's a crafty old bastard. Brass starts making noise about him losing his touch, touting the benefit of retirement and what does he do?" Rutland smirked. "He brings back the prodigal son he never had."

Unwilling to be baited, Guy ignored the provoking comment. "We're eating here, Rutland. Go away."

Rutland bared his crooked teeth in a smile. "I don't have to take orders from you now, *former* Lieutenant Colonel."

Guy set his fork aside and stood. His chair legs scraped the floor as he pushed away from the table and the room around them grew quiet. "You can either go away on your own, or I'll make you."

*Say something*, Guy thought. *Go ahead. I'd love to wail the shit out of you again.*

Rutland sneered at him. "I think you'd find it a lot harder without your buddies. No back up this time. Even odds, eh?"

"Nope," Guy said, moving farther into Rutland's personal space. "Just more opportunities for me to hit you." He smiled. "Off base, again, Rutland, just like old times. Only this time the only person who'd get their ass called on the carpet is you." He paused, letting that little detail sink in. "Like I said, you can either go. Or I'll make you. What'll it be?"

Predictably, Rutland backed down. Fucking coward, Guy thought, adrenaline rushing through his veins.

"Is there a problem, gentleman?" the manager asked.

Guy quirked a menacing brow at Rutland.

"No," Rutland snarled. "I was just leaving." He flashed an evil smile at Guy. "But I'll see you around. Count on it."

Guy glanced at Julia, who was sitting in frozen fascination at their table. Humiliated, no doubt, Guy thought, his own face burning, but with anger. "You ready?"

She nodded shakily. "Er…sure."

He tossed enough cash on the table to cover

the bill, then grabbed her hand and led her out of the restaurant, his thoughts still tangled up with Rutland's parting comment. *Count on it.* Guy didn't have any idea what the asshole had meant, but he knew—*knew*—that he wasn't going to like it. He'd been too damned smug and too damned confident.

And if Garrett had left him out of the loop again, there'd be hell to pay.

ANOTHER UNEXPECTED PERSONAL revelation, Julia thought as they made their way across the parking lot. Evidently she had a bloodthirsty streak because she'd actually been impressed and amazingly turned on by the testosterone show she'd just witnessed.

Her? Sexually excited over the possibility of a fight?

What the hell was happening to her?

She'd pegged Guy for a hell-raising bad ass, the epitome of an alpha male—a modern-day pirate, Julia thought and mercy, she'd always had a weakness for pirates—but watching him morph from charming date to guard dog had been nothing short of amazing. That guy—Rutland, he'd called him—had been a total ass and, after the shock of the confrontation, Julia had been secretly hoping that Guy would deck him.

He was a protector in every sense of the word and that, to her ultimate surprise, was an absolutely thrilling turn on. A sexy irreverent warrior. *Mercy, what a combination.*

Guy'd gotten right up in Rutland's face and looked like he would have not only beat the ever-loving hell out of him, but would have enjoyed doing it. He'd been provoked, he'd stood his ground, then had taken the other guy's.

A rush of heat landed in her womb and she slid him a sidelong glance. Dear God, she was nearly giddy.

"Sorry about that," Guy told her sheepishly as they made their way across the parking lot. He hit the keyless remote, unlocking the doors, then opened hers for her.

Julia slid into the cab of his truck. "Don't

be," she said, still thrumming from the excitement. "It wasn't your fault."

He paused to look at her. "You're not embarrassed?" he asked cautiously.

"Not at all." She grinned, still impressed. "But I'm sure that he is."

Guy paused and cocked his head as though he didn't know quite what to make of her. "My God," he said softly. "You liked that, didn't you?"

"No," Julia lied, blushing. "That would be ghoulish. I didn't like that you were going to get into a fight…but I liked knowing you would win." Talk about hot. That was hot.

He chuckled at her, seemingly bewildered, then climbed behind the wheel.

"Who was that guy, anyway?" she asked. "What did he mean about Garrett and you being the prodigal son he'd never had?"

Dusk was slowing giving way to night, painting the sky in a dark cornflower blue and the absence of light created a cozy intimacy in the small cab of his truck. She watched Guy's jaw harden as he considered her questions.

"That guy was Richard Rutland. He's an ass. And as for what he meant about Garrett… I'm not exactly sure yet." He aimed his truck back toward the base and didn't seem inclined to elaborate.

This was clearly his territory, but from if she'd followed Rutland correctly, it sounded like Garrett's leadership was being called into question. She shared her theory with Guy. "Does that make sense to you?"

Guy nodded. "Garrett's on old warhorse. Hc handpicked our team and our successes were his coup."

"So he's counting on the success of this new team to prove that he's still got it, then?"

He nodded, still lost in his own thoughts. "That sounds like an accurate assessment, yes." Guy swore softly, as though a sudden realization had occurred to him.

From what Julia had been able to make of Guy and Rutland's confrontation, they'd tangled once before and evidently Guy's friends had been part of it. But what had they fought over? What would make them so angry that they'd all three lay into him? Julia wondered. Yes, he was a provoking ass...but three to one? Those were hardly fair odds.

"So you've fought with Rutland before?" Julia ventured, mining for more details. Over a woman maybe?

A muscle ticked in his jaw and he swallowed before responding. "Yes, I have."

Dangerous territory, she could tell, but... "Why?"

"Because he mouthed off about a good friend of mine—a member of my unit who didn't make it back from our last mission—and, since he didn't show proper respect, Payne, Jamie and I decided we should teach him a little." He paused. "Jamie, Payne, Danny and I...we'd been friends since college, met in the ROTC program at the University of Alabama. It was tough losing him."

Julia didn't know what she'd expected him

to say, but that certainly wasn't it. Issues, she remembered. Guy McCann had issues and she'd just learned the source behind them. Her heart squeezed. "I'm sorry," Julia said softly, not altogether sure how to respond.

So that's why he was *former* military then. She could certainly understand that. As team leader, no doubt he felt responsible for the death of his friend, regardless of whether or not he was actually at fault. Men were like that and this one in particular would be, Julia knew.

Guy pulled up in front of the duplex and shifted into park. He looked tired all of the sudden—tense, like he'd been this morning in Garrett's office. He didn't want to be here, Julia realized. If the death of his friend had been bad enough to send him out of the military, then being back here had to be excruciating. So why come back? What had made him leave his new life—the one she imagined he'd created to replace the old damaged one—and do Garrett's bidding?

Julia's lips curled as understanding dawned.

He was here for the same reason she was—to repay a debt.

A snippet of conversation floated back to her, opening another window of insight.

*Off base, again, Rutland, just like old times. Only this time the only person who'd get their ass called on the carpet is you...*

Julia had enough military understanding from her father to know that fighting—particularly off base—was a big no-no.

"What's Garrett got on you?" Julia finally asked, though she had a pretty good idea.

His turned to face her. "What do you mean?"

"You left the military after the death of a good friend. You obviously don't want to be here." She shrugged. "I'm here because my dad owes Garrett. You owe him something, too, right?"

A grim smile rolled around Guy's lips. "You're quick."

"And curious," she said, shooting his line right back at him. "What do you owe Garrett?"

"A favor," Guy said simply. "I gave him a favor in return for my freedom. We all did."

"You mean your other two friends? Who are they again?"

"Jamie Flanagan and Brian Payne. The fight with Rutland put a flag on our clearance papers. Uncle Sam wasn't happy about losing us to start with and that fight… Well, let's just say it could have held us up indefinitely. Garrett made sure that didn't happen and his price was a favor. One from each of us. He's called theirs in already. They're done with him." A weak but determined smile caught the corner of his mouth. "And as soon as I finish out this week, I am, too."

And from the tone of his voice, that couldn't come soon enough.

# 6

*Atlanta*

"I DON'T LIKE THIS," Jamie Flanagan said as he snapped his cell shut. He and Payne currently sat in Samuel's Pub, their usual haunt and his favorite place to get hot wings and good Irish whiskey. Audrey—his increasingly moody and beautifully pregnant wife—was watching a chick flick with Payne's fiancé, Emma. Pleading boredom, Jamie and Payne had escaped to the pub, which was where Guy had finally caught them on Jamie's cell.

"Don't like what?" Payne asked.

"His first day back on base and Guy's already ran into Rutland." Miserable bastard,

Jamie thought. He'd never hated a person more. In fact, he'd never hated anybody but Rutland.

Payne's expression blackened. "I don't like it, either."

"He saw him at Frank's. Said Rutland was being a smug ass."

"That certainly fits his profile." Payne tipped back his beer. "When was he not a smug ass?"

Jamie chuckled and took a drink of whiskey. "He wasn't so smug when we were beating the hell out of him, was he?"

Looking more relaxed than Jamie had ever seen him, Payne grinned, conceding the point. "There is that. But he deserved it."

Jamie had been in his share of fights over the years, particularly when he was younger, but the older he'd gotten, the more he'd learned to control his temper. Rutland had provoked them many times, but the night he'd ran his mouth about Danny had been the last damned straw.

He'd snapped and Guy and Payne had followed suit.

"Guy's convinced that Garrett has left him in the dark again." Payne had already told him about Julia Beckam and passed around her mug shot. Truthfully, they'd all gotten a kick out of it. Leave it to Garrett to pair Guy up with a sentimental how-does-that-make-you-feel? hottie.

Jamie had already gotten married—the best damned decision he'd ever made—and Payne and Emma were unexpectedly tying the knot this weekend and in a unique way—the bride didn't have any idea. Jamie grinned. If Guy brought this Julia Beckam home and kept her, then they were going to all have to thank Garrett, or at the very least nickname him Colonel Cupid.

Jamie selected a hot wing and dipped in a pool of cool ranch dressing. "From what Guy picked up from Rutland, brass is sounding off about Garrett losing his touch and is waving the retirement flag at him."

Payne frowned. "Garrett? Retire? I can't imagine him taking that well."

Him, either, Jamie thought. "That's why he's called in Guy. He pulled together Project Chameleon's replacement team and headlined the former team leader as an instructor." Jamie shrugged and let go a long breath. "My guess is he's trying to prove that he's still got it and Guy's his ace in the hole."

Payne paused consideringly, that cool pragmatic mind working. "If Garrett's hid something else from him, his ace in the hole is going to turn into a friggin' land mine. And I don't know about you, but I wouldn't want to be around when he detonated."

Jamie snorted. "Nobody in their right mind would."

GUY RAPPED LIGHTLY ON Julia's door and waited for her to appear. They'd agreed last night before parting ways that riding together to the educational center made more sense than driving separately. If she hadn't been feeling sorry for him, Guy knew she would have put up an argument. Simply for the sake of argument, he thought with a grin. As it was, though he hated being pitied, he had to admit that he didn't mind that her sympathy had worked to his advantage.

He didn't have any idea how she had slept, but rest hadn't come easy to him last night. Between knowing that she was next door, her hair probably down and practically naked in a nightie, and laboring under the mistaken impression that there was something wrong with her sexual performance... God, how he wanted to remedy that notion for her and his imagination had obligingly called up many different lessons, each one more depraved than the last. Not to mention worrying about conducting this friggin' class today, Guy's nerves were stretched to the breaking point.

Being here was hard enough, made him feel like the ultimate fraud—who was he to teach these boys when he'd betrayed his own team by allowing one of their own to get killed?—but Guy couldn't shake the sensation that the other shoe was about to drop.

And for whatever reason, he suspected the shoe belonged to Rutland.

Guy had replayed last night's exchange over and over and he kept coming back to Rutland's parting comment. *Count on it.* He'd hadn't been simply confident—he'd been certain.

There was a difference.

Guy had called Jamie last night and filled him in on the newest developments and his friend had agreed. Something wasn't kosher, that was for damned sure, and whatever it was would undoubtedly be brought to Guy's attention this morning.

At any rate, he'd reviewed the curriculum again—he and Julia had briefly skimmed things last night when they'd returned from Frank's—and he felt like he was as prepared as he could be, given that he didn't feel like he really had anything to offer.

In his typical maverick form, he'd decided he didn't particularly care for the present outline and would be doing a bit more practical lecturing rather than putting them through a bunch of pointless exercises.

Garrett wanted him to come in here and recreate his team and that simply wasn't going to happen. No amount of team building or advice from Julia on how to build a trusting relationship would duplicate the years of experience, camaraderie and genuine friendship between him, Payne, Jamie and Danny.

The dynamic couldn't be duplicated.

And if Garrett was betting otherwise to keep from being put out to pasture, then he'd better think again.

Hell, they'd been friends for eight years before they'd been selected for Project Chameleon. Though it sounded sentimental, he and his buddies and current business partners were more than friends—they were brothers of the heart.

He knocked again, and within moments, buttoned and "bunned" within an inch of her life, Julia opened the door and smiled at him. Something in his chest gave an unexpected flutter and he found himself inexplicably glad to see her. Odd, that, Guy thought. He couldn't remember the last time he'd been glad to see a woman, if ever.

Though he loved sex as much as the next man, Guy'd always adhered to The Bachelor League rules he, Danny, Payne and Jamie had authenticated in college. Never spend the entire night with a woman, never let her eat off your plate and after the third date cut her loose.

Of course, Payne and Jamie had let those rules go by the wayside recently—quite happily—but Guy couldn't see himself ever settling down. Frankly, though he was careful to keep a tight rein on his temper, he lived with the constant fear that he'd eventually snap and hit his wife, maybe even, God forbid, his child.

Guy had bad blood running through his veins—his bastard father's— and couldn't deny that there were times when his temper erupted and he was grimly reminded of his old man. Guy liked to think that he was a better caliber of man, that he'd never do anything so cowardly and horrible, but in the end, who knew? Payne and Jamie insisted that he'd never do anything so terrible, but Guy figured it was better to never take that chance. He'd already failed one person he'd loved—Danny—and didn't think he could withstand doing anything so gut-wrenching again.

"Good morning," Julia said. She wore a pale yellow linen pantsuit which looked particularly striking with her hair and a rosy gloss covered that amazing mouth.

The tantalizing scent of bacon and some sort of fruity muffin emanated from behind her, making his mouth inexplicably water. Unlike her, Guy hadn't been to the grocery store, so all he'd had to eat this morning was a complimentary cup of coffee. He grimaced. And a piss-poor one at that. His stomach rumbled. Loudly.

"Something smells good," he said, shooting her a hopeful look.

She poked her tongue in her cheek. "Would you like some breakfast?"

"What tipped you off? My blatant fishing for an invitation or my stomach growling?"

"Both. You'll have to hurry, though. I don't want to be late."

Her? Really? He would have never guessed, Guy thought with a droll smile. "No worries. I'll eat fast."

"Have a seat," Julia told him, her mouth curving in a soft knowing grin. Once again that odd unfamiliar little flutter winged through his chest. "I'll fix you a plate."

The last person to fix him a plate had been his mother, Guy realized, curiously warmed by Julia's domestic gesture. And that had been too long ago. He tried to visit at least once a month now that he was out of the service, but things didn't always go according to plan. Janie McCann always took things in stride though, content to count her blessings and be on her own. After eighteen years with a mean drunk prone to believable bouts of repentance, his mother had morphed into a new woman after his father had left.

Guy would never forget that day. His father'd had a bad day at work, had come home early and been instantly enraged because his mother hadn't had his dinner on the table. Evidently pissed that she didn't have the psychic ability to know that he'd be arriving an hour before his usual time, he'd lifted a frying pan with an inch of hot grease in the bottom from the stove and hurled it at her. She still bore the scars.

Tired and sweaty from football practice, Guy had walked in just in time to witness the horror and had instantly lit into his father. Fed up and frightened and furious, he'd pummeled the living hell out of him, and probably wouldn't have stopped if it hadn't been for the coke bottle he'd taken upside the head. His father had snagged it from the counter, and the blow to his temple had knocked Guy out cold.

He'd awakened in a hospital room with thirty stitches in the side of his head, his mother, burned but bandaged, at his side. "He's gone," she'd said with a simple finality that had brought a wave of instant relief.

Hank McCann had never been seen or heard from again, at least not in Burnt Rock, Alabama.

"The coffee will be ready in a minute," Julia said, sliding a plate in front of him. "How do you like it?"

Guy blinked, pulled away from the memory and managed a smile. "Black, thanks." He snagged a piece of bacon. "Do you always cook breakfast?" he asked. He enjoyed it, of course, but never seemed to have the time.

Julia nodded. "I do. My dad was a three-square-meals type, so I got used to having a full breakfast. Every once in a while I'll settle for a muffin, but most of the time I cook. I enjoy it," she said, pulling a small shrug. "So it's no problem."

She set a cup of coffee beside his plate, then tidied the kitchen while he inhaled his food. "That was excellent," Guy told her. A few minutes later, he rinsed off his plate. "Thank you. Do you usually have that many leftovers?" he asked her, shooting her a grin. "'Cause if so, you can count on me finishing things up for you every morning while we're here."

"I thought I might."

"That easy to read, am I?"

That sexy mouth curled around the edges and she quirked a pointed brow. "You're a man, aren't you?" She dried her hands, then looked around the kitchen, presumably to make sure that she hadn't forgotten anything. "We should probably get going."

"Hey," Guy teased, feigning offense. "Don't be insulting my gender." He followed her back to the living room and waited while she collected her purse and attaché case. "What's for dinner, by the way?"

"Chicken Marsala."

"I'm invited, right?"

"That depends."

"On what?"

"I don't know yet, but I thought I'd better qualify it."

He'd give her something to qualify, Guy decided, the little smart-ass. She'd just reached for the doorknob when he snagged her elbow and whirled her around to face him. A startled oomph of air leaked out of her mouth…and promptly into his as he sealed his lips over hers.

*Yum.*

Breakfast had been good, but this was better.

She responded instantly, her mouth going soft and welcoming and there was nothing tentative about her tongue tangling around his. He felt her body quicken with instant desire, then melt against him and his dick instantly went hard, nudging her belly. A tingle started at the nape of his neck and zipped down his spine, making him rock forward against her.

It wasn't nearly close enough.

She whimpered into his mouth, the sound desperate and needy and it vibrated something deep inside of him.

And she thought something was wrong with *her?* Guy marveled again. She was the most responsive woman he'd ever touched—absolutely lit him up—and yet she didn't see it?

Mind-boggling. Absolutely mind-boggling.

He didn't just want to take her—he wanted to *consume* her. He wanted to taste her all over, the side of her neck, the fragrant valley between her breasts, the silky, perfect line of her hip…then feast between her thighs, the softest, sweetest part of her.

Julia tore her mouth from his. "We've…got to…go," she gasped brokenly, her gaze heavy-lidded and darkened with need.

"To the bedroom?"

A helpless chuckle bubbled up her throat. "To work," she said.

"Oh." He rested his forehead against hers, willed his racing pulse to slow and his aching groin to subside. "Have you thought anymore about my offer?"

"What offer?" she asked though he could tell she knew exactly what he was talking about.

"Last night I offered to sleep with you, remember? To prove there's nothing wrong with you."

She giggled. "Vaguely."

"You should probably take me up on that," Guy told her matter of factly.

She smiled and hummed under her breath. "What's in it for me?"

He drew back, a bit startled by the question—possibly because the women he'd had sex with had always anticipated the benefits—but ultimately recovered. She wanted to know what was in it for her? Fine. He'd tell her. Guy lowered his voice. "A night of hard, back-bending, balls-to-the-wall, no-holds-barred wild gorilla sex." He rocked forward, punctuating the promise with a deliberate thrust. "Satisfaction guaranteed."

Julia's gaze darkened even more and a shaky breath leaked gratifyingly out of her lungs. "Oh," she said weakly. "Is that all?"

Guy leaned his head back and laughed. "Baby, if it's not enough then we're in trouble."

SHE WAS ALREADY IN TROUBLE, Julia thought helplessly as every particle in her body thrummed with unfulfilled sexual agony.

Between that bone-melting lip-lock in Guy's truck last night, and the spine-tingling tender kiss he'd given her right before he'd walked over to his side of the duplex when they'd returned from the restaurant, Julia's sexual frustration levels had reached critical mass.

When he'd offered to sleep with her to prove that there was nothing wrong with her sexually, he'd had no idea how close he'd been to her own thoughts. She'd wanted him to sleep with her for completely different reasons, of course—to teach her how to properly have balls-to-the-wall, no-holds-barred wild gorilla sex.

She swallowed a whimper at the mere thought.

Oh, who the hell was she kidding? She wanted to have sex with him because he absolutely tripped every possible trigger she possessed—and some she hadn't known were there. That crooked grin made her belly go all hot and muddled and her brain turn to complete mush. He was gorgeous and

# GET FREE BOOKS and a FREE MYSTERY GIFT WHEN YOU PLAY THE...

*Just scratch off the silver box with a coin. Then check below to see the gifts you get!*

## SLOT MACHINE GAME!

# YES! I have scratched off the silver box. Please send me the 2 FREE books and mystery gift for which I qualify. I understand I am under no obligation to purchase any books, as explained on the back of this card. I am over 18 years of age.

K7KI

Mrs/Miss/Ms/Mr _____ Initials _____

BLOCK CAPITALS PLEASE

Surname _____

Address _____

_____

Postcode _____

| 7 | 7 | 7 | **Worth TWO FREE BOOKS plus a BONUS Mystery Gift!** |
| 🍒 | 🍒 | 🍒 | **Worth TWO FREE BOOKS!** |
| ♣ | ♣ | ♣ | **Worth ONE FREE BOOK!** |
| 🔔 | 🔔 | 🍒 | **TRY AGAIN!** |

*Visit us online at www.millsandboon.co.uk*

## The Reader Service™ — Here's how it works:

THE READER SERVICE™
FREE BOOK OFFER
FREEPOST CN81
CROYDON
CR9 3WZ

NO STAMP
NECESSARY
IF POSTED IN
THE U.K. OR N.I.

charming, wicked and witty and the devil in her recognized the devil in him. He was funny and chivalrous and…and wounded, Julia thought, remembering the haunted look in his eyes when he'd told her about his friend.

Because she was a nurturer by nature and because she felt the inherent need to "fix" everyone, Julia instantly wanted to reach out and help him. His pain tugged at her heart-strings, and his vulnerability somehow made him all the more appealing. It meant he had the capacity to feel—to really care and love—and if she wasn't careful she'd inevitably end up wanting him to care and love her.

And that was guaranteed heartache.

Not exactly what she was looking for with her guaranteed orgasm.

Ultimately, it had occurred to her that she wasn't the only one who needed a lesson. She needed a skilled sexual instructor, and Guy McCann needed to a.) realize that he wasn't responsible for his friend's death and b.) learn to trust himself again.

Because he didn't.

He hadn't told her as much, of course—pride wouldn't allow it—but it was easy enough to see when she read between the lines.

For the time being they needed each other and once Julia had realized that she had something to offer Guy in return for his help—other than her body—she'd decided she'd be a fool not to take advantage of the situation.

Right, wrong or stupid—and two out of three of those were probably accurate—she fully intended to have wild gorilla sex with Guy McCann.

Julia released a slow breath. Business first, pleasure later, she told herself and fished the keys out of her purse. She locked up and started down the sidewalk, Guy and his *satisfaction guaranteed* promise at her back, making her pulse sing in her veins.

"What are you doing?" he asked. "I thought you said we'd ride together."

She blinked innocently and looked from him to her car and back again. "We are."

He paused, a slow-dawning smile sliding across his lips. "In my truck."

"You never said that."

"It was implied."

"I must have missed that."

"*Julia.*"

"Oh, for pity's sake, Guy," she finally said, exasperated. She opened the door and slid behind the wheel. "Just get in the damned car. We're going to be late."

"It's a chick car," he grumbled under his breath. He scooted the seat back and reluctantly climbed inside.

Julia smiled, started the car and pulled away from the curb. "It's a Volkswagon. Men drive them, too."

"Men don't drive Bugs. Especially baby blue ones," he added grimly.

"Men who are confident in their masculinity don't mind."

He grunted under his breath and scowled adorably at the flower in the cup holder of her dash. "Spoken like a true chick."

"Do you want to tell me where we're going?"

He slid her a slightly smug glance. "Where's your map?"

"Beneath your ass."

Guy laughed and looked away. "I can't win, can I?"

Julia felt her lips twitch. "Are we playing a game?"

Guy sighed and his strangely puzzled gaze drifted over her face, making her belly clench. "No, but I think I'm losing anyway."

"Tell me where we going," she said, warmed by that hot green stare.

Guy did and in five minutes they'd pulled into the parking lot. Julia climbed from the car and snagged her attaché case. Guy merely adjusted his shades and seemed to be bracing himself for what was to come.

"I'm looking forward to hearing what you have to say to these guys," Julia told him. "You must have several good stories to tell."

Guy smiled, seemingly recognizing the gesture for what it was—a vote of confidence.

"Some," he conceded. "Come on," he told her, snugging a finger into the small of her back and nudging her forward. "Let's get this over with."

Outfitted in serviceable beige tile and painted cinder block walls, the educational building was functional with no frills. The scent of bleach, sweat and various men's colognes hung in the air and an occasional potted plant offered the vaguest attempt of décor. Guy unerringly led them to their class-room, then with his mouth set in a grim, resigned line, he opened the door for her and ushered her in.

Four men sat in regular classroom chairs at the front of the room and each one of them turned around as they entered.

"Speak of the devil," one of the men said in a heavily sarcastic voice Julia recognized from last night. A gust of dread blindsided her.

*Oh, God.*

*Richard Rutland.*

Behind her Guy went dangerously still. Julia turned around in time to watch him and Rutland lock gazes. Guy's was hard and ominous, while Rutland's seem positively—evilly—delighted.

"Give me your keys," Guy said in a voice so devoid of emotion it practically thundered in the suddenly silent room.

Julia did.

Oy. Apparently men *did* drive baby blue Bugs.

# 7

GLADYS'S MOUTH WORKED up and down in apparent surprise, then she shot up from the chair behind her desk as though she'd been poked in the ass with a straight pin. "Sir— McCann— *Stop!* You can't just barge in there!"

"The hell I can't," Guy said, striding into Garrett's office. "Watch me." The colonel's startled blue gaze swung to his and Guy knew instantly that the older man knew exactly why he was here.

His brow wrinkled into an annoyed line. "McCann—"

Guy planted both fists in the middle of Garrett's desk and leaned forward. "What the hell are you playing at?" His voice was so hard he barely recognized it as his own.

"What do you mean?"

"Fuck it," Guy said, instantly disgusted. He wasn't going to play word games with Garrett. The crafty old bastard knew exactly why he was here and yet he wanted to pretend to be thick? Waste more of his time? His life? Guy drew back and pivoted on his heel. "I'm through. I don't owe you a goddamned thing. Debt paid, Garrett."

Guy heard Garrett's chair slam against the credenza behind his desk. *"Wait."*

Guy didn't know what made him turn around—the fact that Garrett had actually vaulted out of his chair or the slight hint of desperation he heard in the old man's voice. "What?"

Ashen-faced, his brow dotted with perspiration, Garrett gestured toward a chair. "Please hear me out."

Guy crossed his arms over his chest and leaned his back against the door. "I'll stand. You have thirty seconds. Don't mince words

and don't leave anything out. *I. Am. Done.* Do
I make myself clear?"

Clearly shaken, Garrett resumed his seat.
"I'm assuming you're here because of Rutland?"

Guy grunted and felt a smirk roll around his
lips. "That's why you're the colonel. You just
wasted five seconds."

Garrett paused, seemingly at a loss. He
sighed and in that instant he aged ten years
right before Guy's eyes. "He's the best we've
got, McCann. The cream of the crop is in that
room right now and unfortunately—like it or
not—he's part of it."

Guy snorted darkly. "Well, if he's the best
you've got, then you need to scrap this plan altogether because it won't work."

He felt betrayed, Guy realized. He'd always
secretly suspected that Garrett had been proud
of him, Jamie and Payne when they'd put
that arrogant bastard in his place. And yet
he wanted Guy to teach him? Work with a
man who absolutely no respect for his fellow

peers? For the risks they took, the lives which had been lost?

He couldn't do it.

*Wouldn't.*

"I can't scrap it," Garrett said, seemingly agitated. "I need this to work, McCann. That's why I brought you here, dammit. You're the only guy who can make it happen. I have faith in you."

Then that made one of them, Guy thought, smothering a grunt of derision.

"My back's against the wall," Garrett finally—reluctantly—admitted. "If this team isn't successful, I might as well retire."

"Would that be so bad?"

Garrett smiled sadly. "For a man like me? Yes."

The man was old and in fear of becoming a has-been. He'd become the job—it defined him—and retiring clearly meant losing his identity. Guy felt sorry for him, he really did. But favor or not, honor be damned, he couldn't do this. It would never work.

Guy released a pent-up breath and massaged the bridge of his nose. "Colonel, I have always had the utmost respect for you, but I won't work with Rutland—and you know why. Danny was my friend—more than a friend—and I won't help a man take his place who had so little respect for the life he lost." He lifted a shoulder in a negligent shrug. "If he's the best you've got, then we're both wasting our time."

Garrett sighed as though he fully expected Guy's response. "Do you have an alternate suggestion?"

"Eliminate him. Poll the other guys for a replacement. Trust is key here and they'll never trust Rutland, and if they do they're idiots. You know as well as I do that Project Chameleon doesn't have room for idiots."

Furthermore, given Rutland's penchant for running off at the mouth, Guy knew he'd have a helluva time getting them to trust him now. No doubt the mangy SOB had already filled them in on his failure and undermined his authority. Guy mentally swore, his mouth went dry and nausea crept up the back of his throat.

He'd have to tell them about Danny.

Garrett studied Guy, seemed to be weighing his advice.

"This is a deal breaker, Colonel. Who do you need worse—him or me?"

"Send him to me," Garrett said without hesitation. His brows formed an intimidating line. "This had better work, McCann. The remainder of my career is riding on it."

"Trust me. It's the *only* way it'll work."

Satisfied and looking forward to wiping the smug smile off Rutland's face, Guy backtracked across base, parked Julia's little car as close to the building as he could and then made his way back upstairs to the classroom.

In the middle of dispensing handouts, Julia's questioning gaze swung to his as he reentered the room. "—and p-please give it a careful read before coming back to class tomorrow. There's a questionnaire in the back which will help us determine how each of you, on an individual basis, learns to trust."

Guy strolled to the front of the classroom and joined Julia. He felt his lips slide into a smile and his gaze found Rutland's. He paused, savoring the moment. *This is for you, Danny.* Not as good as decking him, but it'd do in a pinch. "Colonel Garrett would like to see you."

Rutland's jaw tensed. "I'll go after class. I'd hate to miss anything *you're* going to teach us."

"Then I'm afraid you'll be hating it. He wants to see you *now*." Guy jerked his head toward the door, dismissing him. "Collect your things and go."

Rutland laughed and shook his head. Hate blazed from his eyes. "Got me bounced, didn't you?"

Guy nodded once and a hard smile curled his lips. *"Count on it."*

From the corner of his eye he caught Julia's pleased expression and for whatever reason, that tiny smile and look of satisfaction in those clear green eyes made him want to beat his chest and roar like a true Neanderthal. She was proud of him, Guy realized, and the idea made him feel positively…wonderful.

Grumbling under his breath, but not loud enough for Guy to understand what he was saying, Rutland gathered his things—loudly, of course—and slammed the door on his way out.

Guy surveyed the other three men in front of him, gauging their response. One guy—O'Malley—according to the white sticky name tag adhered to his shirt—Julia's work, no doubt, he thought stifling a smile—looked openly relieved.

*Jamie, Guy thought.*

His gaze shifted to the next man—Holt. Cool, impassive, the perfect poker face. He kept his own council and you wouldn't know his opinion unless he chose to share it with you.

*Payne.*

Guy surveyed the last man in the room, a dark-haired clear-eyed man named Mitchell who met his gaze directly. Smart, a bit cocky and from the vaguest hint of relief in his gaze, he too was glad to see the backside of Rutland leaving this crew. He smiled at Guy and gave a slight up-nod of appreciation.

*And him,* Guy realized, recognizing the similarities.

"Richard Rutland will no longer be a part of this unit," Guy said. "I've spoken with Colonel Garrett and he's given me permission to poll the three of you for a replacement." He paused, letting the statement sink in. "Any recommendations?"

The three men looked at each other and though no one said a word, Holt finally spoke up. "Jack Anderson."

Guy looked to the other two men. "Anderson is a stand-up guy," Mitchell said, adding his approval.

O'Malley nodded once, indicating a decisive nature. "I'd want him at my back."

"Will he be interested in becoming part of this unit?"

"Definitely," Mitchell told him.

Guy nodded and set his hands at his waist.

"Good. I'll alert Colonel Garrett of the replace-ment and see to it that Anderson reports ASAP." He glanced at each of them in turn. "Any ques-tions?" A thousand hung in the air, but no one voiced any, so Guy merely nodded. "Okay. I'm former Lieutenant Colonel Guy McCann and I was unit commander of Project Chameleon until the death of a good friend of mine."

Better to address it head-on, Guy thought, bracing himself for the confession. He hadn't truly spoken of Danny's death to anyone since it had happened—with Jamie and Payne he hadn't had to. They'd gotten it, had known what he'd been going through without him having to spell it out for them. Words hadn't been neces-sary. Grief had had a language all its own.

"Danny Levinson was killed in action during our last mission. We were ambushed." He paused, swallowed as the memory threat-ened to smother him. "At that point my re-maining unit partners and I decided to leave the military. We currently run a security and P.I. business in Atlanta. I'm here because

Colonel Garrett has asked me to be here. I'm here to share my experience, the good, the bad and the ugly." He smiled. "Welcome to the big leagues, gentleman. Let's get started."

# 8

"HOW'D YOU DO IT?" Julia asked the minute the men left the room. If she sounded impressed, it's because she was.

Guy had been…phenomenal.

She'd realized, of course that becoming a Ranger was no easy task—that only the best of the best were accepted into Ranger school—and that it took a truly spectacular soldier to be selected for a elite special forces team.

But for whatever reason, she hadn't realized that this wounded, irreverent, sexy bad boy had been one of them.

She'd known it…but she hadn't *appreciated* it.

Today she'd gotten a glimpse of the kind of soldier he'd been and the pain he was still dealing with as a result of the death of his friend. His description of the event had been short and to the point, but the pain, anguish and ultimate responsibility she'd heard in his voice had been utterly heart wrenching. It had penetrated her own chest and she'd had to forcibly resist laying her hand upon his sleeve in a gesture of comfort.

He wouldn't accept it, of course, because he didn't feel like he deserved anyone's comfort. Guy was clearly wallowing in the guilt as penance for an accident that he had no way of controlling, and yet experience told her that until he was ready to forgive himself, he wouldn't be receptive to hearing her opinion.

Or anyone else's for that matter.

As for how he'd handled this class, Julia fully understood why Garrett had bet his future career on Guy McCann. He hadn't kept her participation in this class a secret because he hadn't trusted Guy—he'd done it to *ensure* his participation. He'd needed him that desperately.

Without the slightest discernible hesitation, Guy had walked right in and commanded the room, but more importantly, he'd waded into a bad situation and commanded the respect of this new up-and-coming team. The relief of having Richard Rutland walk out of this room had been practically palpable, then putting the decision of the replacement in their hands had been a pure stroke of genius.

Talk about building instant trust, Julia thought, smiling at Guy.

He paused and a crooked grin spread across that incredibly sexy mouth. Her nipples tingled, just looking at him. "What?" he asked.

"What what?"

"You're staring at me."

Julia shrugged. "I asked you a question and am still waiting for a response."

He arched a brow.

"How did you do it? How did you get rid of Rutland?"

Guy shrugged. "I gave Garrett my professional opinion—"

She'd just bet he did, Julia thought, wishing like hell she could have witnessed that.

"—and he decided that he should listen to me."

She leaned a hip against the desk and regarded him with amusement. "You threatened to walk out, didn't you?"

Guy flashed a smile at her. "It's possible."

"Probable, I'd say."

He sidled closer to her, purposely crowding into her personal space. A sigh leaked out of her lungs, making her quivering belly deflate like a spent party balloon. "You think you've got me all figured out, don't you?"

Julia rolled her eyes. "You're an idiot wrapped in a moron. I would never presume to try and figure you out."

He jerked his head in one of those confident up-nods. "Maybe so…but you want me."

She flattened her lips to keep from smiling. Geez, Lord had she ever met a guy with any more confidence? "You're awfully full of yourself."

His eyes twinkled with wicked humor. "You could be full of me, too, if you'd just say the word."

An image of Guy McCann, naked, hot, needy and hard, poised between her thighs, nudging deep leaped instantly to mind, making her womb clench and soaking her panties with wet, moist heat. "Wh-what word?" Julia asked a little breathlessly.

He leaned forward and planted a lingering sweet kiss on her terrible nose, causing a rush of emotion to clog in her throat. He probably had no idea what he'd just done— how much that tender gesture had meant— and yet Julia knew it was the beginning of the end for her. A few more days in his company and she'd be head over heels in love, planning happily-ever-afters and 'til-death-do-us parts.

Crazy, when she knew he was a player. That's why she'd picked him, right? Because he was so damned good at catch and release.

"*Now*," Guy told her meaningfully. "The

word is now. And the instant you say it, baby, I'll prove to you that there's absolutely nothing wrong with you. Eeyore and those other bastards have got it all wrong," he said, sliding a finger down the side of her face. "You are…" He paused, seemingly searching for the right words. "You are so damned sexy I've kept a perpetual hard-on since the minute I saw you. I look at you and the first thing I want to do it pull that hair down, strip you naked, then back your delectable ass up against the wall and take you until we both scream. I want to taste every part of you—white parts, pink parts and all parts in between." He leaned in and kissed her hard, leaving no room for any error in her mind. It was thrilling and wonderful and she so desperately wanted to believe him. "One word," he repeated softly. "And I'm yours."

Julia blinked drunkenly, trying to reassemble her thoughts. *I'm yours…* Now there was a heady, almost irresistible thought. Guy McCann—Lieutenant Wicked—*hers*.

Seemingly recognizing that coherent

thought had completely abandoned her, Guy grinned at her. "What was that word again?"

"Now."

His gaze darkened. "Excellent. I thought you'd never ask."

Before she fully realized what he was about, he shut the classroom door and locked it with a purposeful click.

"Wait, Guy. I—"

"You said now," he said, sidling swiftly back to her. "Don't you remember?" Those clear green eyes tangled with hers, effectively snatching the breath from her lungs, and the next second he was on her.

His kiss was hot and frantic, thrilling and impatient, all those things she felt herself, hammering away inside her veins, making her utterly insane with need.

With every skilled thrust of his tongue into her mouth, Julia felt a resulting tug in her womb and she no longer gave a damn that they were in a deserted classroom with annoyingly bright fluorescent bulbs overhead.

All that mattered was this moment—the time—with Guy.

An impressive bulge nudged her belly, branded her, and her lips slid into a grateful smile. Perpetual hard-on, indeed Julia thought dimly, no longer concerned that she'd been tricked into saying his one word.

*Now, now, now.*

He *did* want her.

And he could fix her.

She felt his fingers push into her hair, removing pins, until the heavy weight of it fell down over her shoulders.

A masculine hum of pleasure resonated in their joined mouths as he twined a lock around his finger. Julia's feminine muscles clenched and a rush of warmth coated her folds, making her press her sex more firmly against his. Need and instinct took over and she squirmed against him, desperate for that guaranteed orgasm he'd promised her.

Guy tore his mouth from hers, then trailed thorough but speedy kisses down the side of her neck, along her jaw. Julia untangled her fingers from the close-cropped hair at his nape, eagerly jerked his shirt from the waistband of his slacks, then sighed with pleasure when her hands found his bare skin.

Warm, supple and smooth.

Sweet Jesus.

A low masculine hum of pleasure hissed out of him, and his belly shuddered gratifyingly beneath her questing greedy fingers. Getting beneath the shirt wasn't enough—she wanted it off. She wanted to feel those muscles, map the intriguing terrain with her hands until she'd learned every inch of him. She tugged the garment over his head, then tossed it carelessly to the floor.

With a soft wicked chuckle, Guy slowly unbuttoned her shirt, carefully baring her to his gaze. His hot gaze fastened on her chest and she had the pleasure of watching his eyes darken further, a beautiful mossy green. An unsteady breath puffed past his lips as he traced the lacy edge of her bra with slightly shaking fingers.

"It clasps in the front," Julia told him, just in case he hadn't noticed.

"Convenient," he murmured thickly. He slipped his fingers beneath the fastener and gave it a gentle pop. The cups parted and dropped away, baring her taut nipples to his hungry gaze.

"Simply gorgeous," he murmured to her unending delight, then he let go a shaky breath, and lifted her from the waist, gently depositing her onto the desktop. Then he bent his gorgeous head and fastened his greedy mouth onto her aching peak, expertly palmed the other, lest it feel neglected.

Julia gasped with pleasure and sagged beneath the weight of the exquisite torment. He suckled, kissed, licked and ravished. His tongue blazed a trail from peak to peak, alternately around each globe, then pulled each in turn deep into his hot mouth.

*God help her.*

A steady throb built between her legs, then an unfamiliar itchy sensation intensified deep in her womb and she hooked her legs around his thighs, trying desperately to find some sort of relief. She wanted that weighty pressure, desperately needed to feel that hard part of him between her legs. Shameless? Yes. But she was past caring.

It had been too damn long. Too long. And he was...*amazing*.

Julia reached out and scored his muscled chest—his nipples—with her nails, leaned forward and nipped his powerful shoulder, then licked the place where she'd bitten, savoring the salty tang of his skin. His scent invaded her nostrils, dark and seductive, all musk and man.

She squirmed closer to him, let her hand drift over his belly, then boldly stroked his groin. A hot thrill snaked through her at the intimate contact. He was gloriously hard, electrifyingly huge. She slipped the button of his pants from its closure, then felt his warm breath blow over her aching nipple as she lowered his zipper. Less than a second later she had him in hand, tenderly working the hot, slippery flesh over his rigid length. She ran the pad of her thumb over his wet tip, then painted his engorged head with the evidence of his desire. Guy jerked, shuddered, beneath her ministrations, and a low growl of warning issued from his throat.

She felt his warm fingers against her belly, felt her pants give way beneath his questing hands. She wiggled as his hot mouth found hers once more.

A wicked, probing kiss, the dizzying rasp of his tongue against hers. He suckled and stroked, feeding at her until her head suddenly felt too heavy for her neck.

Guy tugged at her pants and she lifted her hips to accommodate him, then impatiently kicked the garments aside. He withdrew a condom from his wallet, swiftly tore into the package with his teeth, then rolled the protection into place.

Julia blinked slowly, astonished at his sheer size, and another thick warm rush of heat seeped into her weeping folds. Her nipples tingled once more and the air in her lungs virtually evaporated, causing her breathing to go shallow. Anticipation made her belly tremble violently.

Guy's warm hands grasped her hips, scooted her forward. The first nudge of him between her nether lips made Julia inhale sharply—then he smoothly slid inside her, buried every glorious inch of himself as far into her as he could—and she exhaled in sublime wonderment. The storm which had been brewing inside her briefly abated, seemingly in awe of the flawless perfection of this moment. It didn't matter that they were locked in a classroom, that her panties had disappeared beneath the desk or that Guy's slacks were sagging around his ankles.

Nothing matter but him being inside her—*finally*.

Guy expelled a harsh breath and he rested his forehead against hers, locking himself inside her as though he never wanted to leave. His hands came up and gently framed her face, then with a tender heart-wrenchingly sweet look, he lowered his mouth to hers once more.

One moment of tenderness in a hurricane of mindlessness was all it took for her silly heart to melt like a drop of water on a hot griddle.

A curiously relieved laugh stuttered out of her mouth and he caught it in his. She looped her arms around his neck, threw every ounce of passion she possessed into the kiss and simultaneously clamped her greedy muscles around him.

Pleasure barbed through her, and the single wanton act was all it took to make Guy forget about being tender. His palms slid down her sides, grazed the margins of her breasts, then wound around until her bottom rested in his big warm hands. He kneaded her rump as he slid in and out of her, a hot thrilling game of seek and retreat that quickly stoked the fire raging through her blood.

A coil of tingly heat tightened in her womb and her breathing came in sharp little puffs as he upped the tempo.

This was it, Julia realized. She was going to come. Really, truly, while Guy was inside of her...*come*.

He pumped harder, faster, then harder still.

Guy's breathing grew labored, as well, and a fine dew of sweat glistened on his shoulders. He pumped in and out of her, a rhythmic, erotic bump and grind that made her nipples quiver and dance as a result of his frantic, manic thrusts.

Julia couldn't get enough of him. Her hands mapped his body. His shoulders, his belly, the small of his back and, when the first sparker of beginning release detonated in her sex, she attached her hands to his perfect ass and writhed wildly against him.

Guy growled low in his throat, a masculine sound of pleasure that sang in her veins.

"Guy," Julia hissed brokenly. "I need— I'm almost—"

With a determined cocky smile, Guy increased his rhythm, pounded even harder into her. One hand left her bottom, came around and massaged her tingling clit. The shock of sensation rent a soundless wail from the back of her throat, and few clever strokes later she came so hard she honestly feared she might lose consciousness. Her vision blackened around the edges, colors faded, bathing the bright room in black and white, and if he hadn't held her tightly against him, she would have undoubtedly slid off the desk and puddled into the floor.

Wave after wave of glorious release eddied through her, tugging her under, pushing her up. Heightened sensation bolted through her with every eager spasm of the orgasm.

She heard Guy's breath catch in his throat, felt him tense, then a low keening growl sounded next to her ear as three hard thrusts later, he joined her in paradise. A shock of warmth pooled against the back of her womb, sending another tingle of joy through her.

To her unreasonable delight, Guy didn't immediately withdraw from her, but rather lingered between her legs.

He braced one hand on the desk, then tipped her chin up. His eyes sparkled with latent humor and lingering lust, and just a hint of something else. Affection, maybe? "I told you we'd have back-bending wild gorilla sex," Guy told her. *"You were fantastic."* A shaky laugh rumbled up from his chest. "There is nothing wrong with you and if you're still not convinced, then I'll simply have to have sex with you again."

Julia smiled, still vibrating from her first major orgasm in years. "Just say the word," she told him.

# <u>9</u>

"SO WHAT'S YOUR FIRST impression of Anderson?" Julia asked. She took a long roundabout lick around the base of her ice cream cone and strolled beside him, completely unaware of the fact that she was absolutely tearing him up. Probably because her tongue had been giving his dick a similar treatment just last night.

*Silky hair sliding over his thighs, warm hand massaging his balls and her hot, hungry mouth sucking at him.*

Dull in the sack, my ass, Guy thought. She was *phenomenal*.

His dick leaped in his jeans, strained toward her like a damned divining rod.

He wanted to track down Warren and every

other miserable shit who'd ever made her feel inadequate and pummel the hell out them. Julia was perfect—an amazing lover—and the fact that she'd ever doubted herself made Guy want to constantly reassure her.

Their second day of class had passed without incident and, though he'd spent entirely too much time thinking about the amazing ball-shrinking sex they'd had on the desk, Guy had to admit he thought things were going pretty well.

They'd done an orienteering trust-building exercise this morning which this new team had completed in a very impressive time. Not as good as theirs had been, of course, he thought with a smile, but within fifteen seconds. Pretty damned good, he had to admit.

As for Anderson…

The man instantly put him in mind of Danny, even had the auburn hair and quirky sense of humor. Guy's chest ached, just thinking about his friend. Anderson exhibited the best qualities of all the men and he was clearly a devoted member of their crew. After a moment, Guy managed to say as much. "He's going to do well."

"I wonder why Garrett went with Rutland instead of Anderson to start with," Julia mused. "Honestly, it's obvious that he's a much better guy."

Payne'd had a theory on that and after further reflection, Guy was fully inclined to agree with him. "I think Garrett put Rutland in that classroom to get me fired up and invested in making this team work," Guy told her.

Julia paused, turned to face him. "Surely not," she breathed softly. A frown wrinkled her otherwise smooth brow. "You think he'd be that damned sneaky?"

Guy pulled an offhand shrug, took a pull from his milk shake. "He didn't get where he's at without being able to shake some things up."

Julia took another long lick of her cone, seemed to be pondering what Guy had just shared. "Well, if that was his angle, then it was a stroke of genius because it worked." She slid him a look. "There was a marked difference between the man you'd been the first time you walked into that classroom and the man you were when you came back. You were confident, purposeful and direct—all qualities designed to instill trust and demand respect." Seemingly impressed, she darted him another speculative look, one of many he'd been getting recently. "You're a badass," she said, eyes twinkling. "A modern-day pirate."

Startled at the somewhat dramatic comparison, Guy chuckled. He'd been called a badass before, but… "A pirate?"

She grinned. "There are similarities."

"Like what?"

"A certain recklessness and disregard for the rules, for starters."

He inclined his head. "Rules are boring."

She laughed. "Spoken like a true pirate."

"It sounds like you've given this a lot of thought."

"Not necessarily," Julia hedged and he could tell that she was lying. For whatever reason, that she'd put so much thought into his character made him feel...special, he realized. She wouldn't waste her time thinking about him if she wasn't interested in the kind of man he was. If she didn't enjoy his company beyond the sex.

Julia gazed around the base, seemingly drinking in the atmosphere. Though it was early spring, the air still held enough heat to make his skin sting. "I like it here," she said. "What's this area of the base called again?"

"Harmony Church," Guy told her. "Both Sniper and Ranger schools are housed in this area of the base."

"Do you miss it?" she asked, sighing softly. "The routine, the purpose? Being part of the cause and the greater good?"

Guy watched a group of guys dressed in BDU's walk by and thoughtfully considered the question. Did he miss it? he wondered, trying to filter the emotional aspect of Danny's death out of the equation.

"To some degree, yes," Guy admitted, surprising himself. "I miss the atmosphere, the thrill of the mission, of being the best of the best." He sighed. "But the best part of being in the military was being with my friends and honestly, I've still got that. Ranger Security isn't as exciting as orchestrating a hostage mission, but then I've got better odds of surviving, as well." He chuckled softly. "Jamie and Payne…they're great. Is this where I thought I'd be now? No. But I'm happy with the outcome." He tangled his fingers in hers and tugged playfully. "What about you?" he wanted to know. "Are you where you want to be right now? Is your ten-year plan lining up for you?" he teased.

Julia chuckled softly and shot him a look. "How did you know I had a ten-year plan?"

Guy laughed. "Oh, baby, you are a stick-to-the-plan kind of girl if I've ever seen one. And a five-year plan would be too short-sighted for you."

Julia chewed the inside of her cheek. "Well, a plan is good," she said, nodding primly. "It forces a person to set goals and adhere to them and encourages critical thinking." Warming to her topic, she paused to look at him. "You know, it wouldn't hurt you to—"

Guy tugged her around and planted a silencing kiss on her mouth to prevent the lecture. She tasted like chocolate ice cream and hot, sweet sex and his heart gave an odd little jolt as she melted readily against him. She was warm and responsive and so damned sexy it was all he could do to keep his hands off of her.

But admittedly, since yesterday afternoon, he hadn't done much of that.

He and Julia had shared lunch, then he'd given her a brief tour of the base. They'd parted company long enough for him to contact Payne and shower, then he'd walked over to her duplex and spent the remainder of the evening with her.

She'd cooked a fabulous meal…then he'd made a meal of her.

Guy had awoken at three o'clock, a bit disoriented from the surroundings, then had glanced over and seen Julia lying beside him. Long, pale golden hair fanned out over her pillow—God, that was sexy—her hand tucked beneath her cheek. She'd been heart breakingly beautiful and something in his chest had shifted, forcing him to release a pent-up breath, one he hadn't realized he'd been holding.

His first instinct had been to curl up next to her, drag her closer to him—her rump to his groin and a plump breast beneath his hand— but Guy hadn't. The fact that he'd even wanted to had scared the living hell out of him—he'd never been tempted to spend the whole night with a woman—and he'd quietly kissed her cheek, murmured a goodbye so she wouldn't feel abandoned, and then made the return trek to his side of the duplex.

Once there, Guy'd had to fight the immediate impulse to go directly back and crawl back into bed with her. His seemed too big, too lonely, and considering he'd never been lonely a day in his life, Guy knew he was wading into uncharted waters he wasn't altogether sure he wanted to explore, pirate or not.

What had started out as a severe case of attraction for him had swiftly morphed into something Guy found himself unable to label. He'd never met anyone like Julia, someone who affected him the way she did. Being with her made him feel better about himself. He enjoyed saying things that shocked her and watching those leaf green eyes widen in impressed outrage. She admired him, Guy thought—genuinely respected him—and knowing that he affected her that way made him feel even better about himself.

Granted he'd never been low in the confidence department—frankly he'd survived too much, accomplished too much—to ever be anything but overconfident. But something about Julia Beckam, in particular, made him feel like a better man.

He wasn't altogether sure what their plans would be at the end of the week when it was time to go back to Atlanta. Despite the fact that he'd be breaking every bachelor rule, a part of him desperately wanted to pursue this relationship once they went back home.

He wanted her to come over and meet his friends, sit on the couch with him and watch a Braves game, share a beer down at Samuel's Pub. He wanted her to stand barefoot in his kitchen in one of his shirts and cook him one of those trademark amazing meals in his designer kitchen which had never helped prepare anything more than a frozen dinner or a Pop-Tarts.

He wanted to get Bear's reaction to her—dogs were a good judge of character in his opinion—and see if he and his canine roommate felt the same way about her.

In short, he was becoming increasingly aware—and increasingly terrified—that he wanted her.

And that had never been part of his ten-year plan.

"WHERE ARE WE GOING AGAIN?" Julia asked, trying once more to get Guy to tell her where they were headed. They'd parked—his truck, of course, she thought with a smile—about half a mile back at Red Diamond Road and had been hiking across a meadow for about ten minutes. Ever the gentleman, Guy blazed a path in front of her making sure she didn't get snakebitten or inadvertently fall into a hole.

"God, woman, how many times do I have to tell you that it's a surprise?"

"That depends on when you stop telling me it's a surprise and tell me where we're going."

He shifted the picnic basket he'd arranged himself from one hand to the other and paused, seemingly getting his bearings.

"We're lost, aren't we?" She knew they weren't of course, she simply enjoyed needling him. She loved it when he got all outraged and cocky. It turned her on. Julia sighed, recognizing the fact that she was way in over her head. But then when did he not turn her on?

Guy turned around, chuckled darkly and shot her a look. "Me? Lost? I was a *Ranger,* for chrissakes. I'm never lost."

Hiding a smile, Julia plucked a bloom of Queen Ann's Lace and twirled it between her fingers. "Okay then. Are you in absence of the knowledge of where we are?"

He grunted. "Say it however you want to, baby, but I am not lost." He started forward once more and she was left with no other choice than to mush along after him. Of course, the view was particularly wonderful— he had a particularly fabulous ass—so she could hardly complain.

Furthermore, he'd told her that they'd be hiking about a mile off road, so she'd worn the right shoes, but she still didn't have any idea where he was taking her. She thought longingly of the map sitting in the front seat of her car and wished she'd consulted it a little more closely.

If she remembered correctly, they were close to Victoria Pond, the area where the amphibious training for the Bradley Fighting Vehicles took place. Since he'd packed a picnic and, that didn't seem particularly romantic, Julia didn't think that's where they were headed.

Quite honestly, it didn't matter because she grimly suspected that she'd follow him anywhere. The past few days with him had been... *indescribably wonderful*. Tomorrow morning they would finish their final class with the new group and then she and Guy would head back to Atlanta, separately...and separated.

He hadn't said a word about continuing their relationship beyond this week and Julia had too much pride to mention it herself. Her pirate was allergic to permanent relationships and she'd known that from the get-go. It had been part of the reason she'd allowed herself to become his sexual pupil, though quite honestly, other than learning how to balance one leg on a toilet seat while hanging on to the wall support in the handicapped stall of the bathroom, she could honestly say that she hadn't exactly discovered anything new.

Evidently, he'd been right. She'd never been the problem, she'd just make the retarded repeated mistake of hooking up with men who didn't know what they were doing.

A warm flutter winged through her belly and settled in her sex.

Guy certainly hadn't had any trouble taking care of her, that was for sure.

In fact, she grimly suspected that he'd spoiled her, what with his bone-melting kissing and multiple orgasms. And God, that wicked smile. Julia let go a shuddering breath. She saw it in her dreams.

*Satisfaction guaranteed.* Too bad it didn't come with a lifetime warranty.

"Ah," Guy said. "There it is."

Intrigued, Julia peered around him and saw a small probably Civil War–era cemetery, judging by the mossy gray stones. A delighted sound of surprise slipped past her lips and her gaze tangled with Guy's. He grinned at her, evidently pleased with himself and her response.

"Like it?" he asked.

Tucked into a rolling meadow of tall grass, the stones seemed lonely but worthy of reverence and Julia found herself inexplicably drawn closer. There was something hauntingly beautiful about old graveyards and she'd always loved doing rubbings—she'd even framed several—and searching for intriguing epitaphs. She'd come across several which had stayed with her over the years—a simple *"She was murdered"* to *"He looked up the elevator shaft to see if a car was coming. It was."*

Guy couldn't have known that strolling through old graveyards and cemeteries was a favorite pastime of hers—she loved the history, the stories told by the births and deaths of those who'd gone before her—and yet he couldn't have taken her anywhere on this base that would have delighted her more.

He set the picnic basket down and joined her as she walked slowly through the listing stones, scanning the inscriptions for interesting names and bits of history. *Seth, Ephraim, Sarah*. Her heart squeezed when she saw a smaller stone. *A stillborn baby*.

"This is beautiful," Julia said softly because this place deserved the quiet regard.

"I liked it," Guy told her. "I had a hunch that you would, too."

"I do," Julia confirmed. She tucked her hand in his and sidled closer to him. "Thank you."

He smiled, seemingly pleased and his woefully familiar green gaze traced a path over her face, almost as though committing it to memory. "You're welcome."

"How did you find out about this place? It's a little off the beaten path."

He grinned, reached down and cleared a clump of weeds away from one of the monuments. "I'm surprised you didn't see it. It's on the map."

Julia chuckled. "So that's how you found it? The map?"

"No." He shoved a hand in his front pocket. "I don't know. Someone mentioned it was out here. It's a good place to think. I used to come here a lot." He paused. "Danny did, too. It's quiet."

Julia paused and watched him scan the stones again, his face an impassive mask and yet she instinctively knew that he'd spent a lot of time here *after* Danny died. He was sharing something special with her, Julia realized. A guarded part of himself.

Her gaze turned inward, remembering the tattoo she'd seen on his right shoulder—an image of an eagle with a ribbon and the inscription *In Memory of Danny Boy* trailing from its beak. When she'd slid a finger over it, he'd tensed, but had told her that Payne and Jamie had the same one, as well. So they never forgot. Honestly, Julia didn't think any of them would ever be in any danger of that.

She cleared her throat. "Your friend must have had good taste."

Guy chuckled. "God, no. Not all the time, anyway," he clarified. "Payne comes from a wealthy family and he's managed his investments well. Like me and Jamie though, Danny's family was just above the poverty line and when he started making pretty decent money, he had a penchant for buying g-gaudy jewelry." Guy chuckled, remembering and shook his head.

"We used to call him pimp daddy, particularly when he wore the pinky ring."

Julia laughed. "Well, he had good taste in friends, at any rate."

Guy's gaze tangled with hers. "He would have liked you," he told her.

No doubt she would have liked him, as well, Julia thought, warmed by the compliment. She tucked her hair behind her ear and waded through the grass.

"Are you hungry?" Guy asked.

Julia grinned. "Have you noticed me missing any meals?"

"Come on," he said, eyes twinkling adorably. "I'll spread a blanket...and we'll feast."

Actually, Julia decided, shooting him a glance, she'd rather feed another appetite. Guy snagged a quilt from the basket and expertly laid it on the ground, then he plopped down and found a comfortable position on his side. He propped his head up with his hand and the devil's own curve slid over his sexy lips.

Julia sighed, recognizing the ploy for

exactly what it was. Masculine wiles. How the hell could she resist? She toed her shoes off, then cocked a pointed brow. "Guy?"

He blinked innocently at her. "Yes?"

*"Now."*

# 10

*Now.*

In this instance Guy didn't think a better word had ever been invented. In fact, given the frequency that Julia had begun to use the simple word, Guy had come to the conclusion that *now* was his favorite word.

Particularly considering that their time together was growing increasingly shorter. Tomorrow at noon they'd wrap up their training session and the idea that she was going to walk out of his life, never to return absolutely made a dead weight sit in his chest.

He'd wanted to do something special with her—*for her*—before they left and had instinctively known that this place would appeal to her. Like him she had a deep appreciation

for history, for imperfect things with a past—
like him, Guy thought—and the look on her
face when she'd seen the cemetery had been
worth every bit of effort he'd put into planning
this picnic for her.

Actually, he'd picked up the sandwiches
and beer at a deli—he'd smiled at the clerk and
she'd even packed it for him—so when it came
to actual effort, he hadn't expended much. But
he'd given her a little piece of himself by
sharing this place with her and because she
was smart and insightful, she'd recognized the
gesture for what it was.

Knowing that he preferred her hair down,
she'd started wearing it that way the past
couple of days and a pale blond curtain of
silky hair fell over her shoulders and down the
middle of her back. She settled herself beside
him and Guy twirled a long lock of that hair
around his finger—his chest tightened as
though it was actually winding around his
heart—and he tugged her to him for a long,
slow kiss.

Sweet heaven, but she tasted good. Warm and willing and sweet and perfect. She tasted like a future, were he willing to have one with her, Guy thought, then forced the fanciful notion away, tempted. He slowly unbuttoned her shirt, baring her body to his hungry gaze and released a shuddering breath as the front clasp of her bra gave way and freed her glorious breasts.

Guy bent and sucked a rosy nipple into his mouth, the taste of her exploding on his tongue. God, how he loved her body. It was long and lean, smooth, soft and firm, a breathtaking combination of sweet curves, intriguing valleys. Pale skin, golden curls, rosy nipples. That beautiful hair fanned out on the blanket like a skein of fine silk.

She was, without a doubt, perfect in every sense of the word.

"You are so beautiful," Guy told her, moving to the other plump breast. "So responsive," he murmured.

Julia arched up, pushing her breast across

his lips once more and shimmied her pants and panties down her legs.

"You're beautiful, too," she told him, her darkened gaze tangling with his, her voice rusty with desire. "I look at you and something happens to me here," she said rubbing a hand over her mound. "I get all hot and achy—hollow—and I can't think about anything but you filling me up. You inside me."

Her foggy tones wrapped around his senses and she leaned forward and nipped at his neck, causing a shower of sensation to trickle over his skin. She lifted her hips once more, a silent plea, then her hands went to work on his clothes, swiftly disrobing him. His jeans and T-shirt joined her own, a discarded pile of forgotten trappings.

Warm hands, a cool breeze and the swish of tall grasses wrapped around them, swaddling him into a memory Guy knew he'd visit frequently when this time with her was over.

She slid her palms over his chest, scoring his nipples, then she massaged his shoulders and drew him back down for another mind-blowing kiss. She sucked at his tongue, the move bold and erotic—like her, Guy thought, loving every second of her sweet seduction.

He bisected her middle with his finger, then slid the pad of his thumb over her clit, causing her to arch up against his hand. She whimpered, enjoying the torture, but he knew she wanted more.

"Guy, please— I need— I want— *Now.*"

In an instant he was sheathed in a condom, positioned between her legs and a half a second later—though it had felt like an eternity—he was sliding between her pink folds, then dipping into her, teasing her. Instinctively her feminine muscles clamped around him, attempting to trap him, draw him in. His dick throbbed with pleasure and he felt the beginning tingle of a climax stir in his loins, tighten his balls.

Too soon, Guy thought.

He dipped again, this time lingering a moment before withdrawing, savoring the feel of her tight heat fisting hard around him.

Julia's neck bowed, exposing her delicate throat, and her mouth opened in a silent moan of ecstasy. She arched beneath him, lifted her hips and rocked, then slid her hands up over his belly, grazed his midsection and scoured his masculine nipples with those neat, manicured feminine nails.

Talk about a turn-on.

He shuddered, closed his eyes, and only by sheer dent of will did he manage *not* to collapse on top of her, push himself so deeply inside her it would take a serious tow package to drag him out.

He pushed again, this time surrendering, and buried himself deeply inside her. A sublime smile of satisfaction curled her kiss-swollen lips and her lids fluttered shut beneath the weight of pleasure. She didn't just want him, Guy realized, she had to have him—the same way he had to have her.

Seeing her reaction, feeling the absolute flawlessness of being inside her, made Guy's his own eyes too heavy and they drifted shut as well. He set his jaw as the matchless perfection of being inside her suddenly consumed him.

She was— She was— Words ultimately failed him. His throat clogged, his heart pounded out an odd rhythm in his chest and, were his toes not firmly planted into the blanket, they would have undoubtedly curled.

Julia clamped around him again, rocked her hips, a silent but effective request and because he wanted nothing more at the moment than to lay in this meadow and make love to her for the rest of his life, he set everything else aside and concentrated on being her pirate—and he'd start by stealing an orgasm from her.

With a deliberate flex, he withdrew and plunged into her again. Found a slow rhythm, savoring the resistance, the perfect draw and drag of their joined bodies. She drew her legs back and attached them to his waist, then reached around and cupped her warm hands over his ass, squeezing, urging, a mewl of carnal pleasure, a purr of satisfaction. She matched him thrust for thrust, easily, as though they'd done this hundreds of times, finding his pace, keeping it, then demanding more.

He felt her tighten around him, then her voice caught, and she upped the tempo. She sank her teeth into her bottom lip, whimpered and thrashed, the fever driving her mindless. Whereas seconds ago she'd been boneless and limp, now she'd gone rigid and wild, desperate for the orgasm Guy firmly intended to serve up. Previous lovers had left her wanting, but not him. He'd take her until his balls burst before he'd let her leave his arms unsatisfied.

His own loins were experiencing the fiery torments of the damned and every cell in his body was ready for release. The instant she caught hers, Guy knew he'd come.

He wrapped an arm around her waist, then pumped frantically, pistoned in and out of her until he thought for sure that his heart would explode. Her feminine muscles clamped again, heralding her impending climax.

A long keening cry tore from her throat. Her body bowed off the blanket, bucked beneath him and the walls of her tight sex collapsed forcefully around him.

And that was all it took to make him explode like a nuclear bomb, pleasure imploding upon itself. She spasmed hard around him, flexed and quivered, and with each pulse he felt himself quake even harder inside her. Her climax perfectly sapped his, draining him of everything but the unmatched satisfaction of *phenomenal* back-bending wild gorilla sex.

When the very last pulse throbbed out of him, Guy gently withdrew, then collapsed next to her and rolled her up firmly next to his side. He draped the blanket over them, watched a butterfly drift lazily from the wildflowers blooming in the meadow.

Her head lay nestled against his chest, her hair spilling over and tickling his side. She rested her sweet palm upon his abdomen, and slung a smooth leg over his thigh. In short, she melted over him like hot caramel over a scoop of ice cream and he didn't know when he'd ever felt anything more remarkable—altering—in his life.

Heart still pounding, Guy bent and pressed a kiss on top of her head, then looked up at the clear blue sky and felt a wash of contentment bathe over him.

Dammit, he shouldn't be feeling this—shouldn't be wanting her the way he did. Needing her. He was a bachelor, dammit, committed to his lifestyle of...what? Guy wondered suddenly.

*Of nothing.*

Work, friends, mother and a dog. The K.I.S.S. approach to life—Keep It Simple Stupid.

"Guy?"

He swirled his fingers on her upper arm. "Hmm?"

A slow sigh slipped past her lips. "Thank you for everything this week. I needed... Well, you know exactly what I needed and you gave it to me and I'm..." He felt her swallow. "I'm grateful." She paused. "And I'm going to miss you."

His chest tightened, forcing him to swallow, as well. He knew he should say something—she'd opened herself up to him—and yet he couldn't find the words. Or at least not the right words because everything he wanted to say was the exact opposite of what he knew was ultimately right.

He wanted to say "I'll miss you, too" or "Why miss me? This doesn't have to be over." But those were the words of a man looking for a committed relationship, of a man who ultimately longed for a family and someone to come home to in the evenings.

Until this week, Guy had never wanted anything remotely resembling that and yet a few days with Julia and he found himself longing for things he'd long ago decided would never be right for him. Bad blood, he'd always told himself. Why risk it?

Resisting the idea had been easy because up until now he'd never met a woman who awakened those kinds of feelings inside him. He'd never wanted the honey-I'm-home fantasy. Never wanted to see another girl past his three date limit. He'd already had more than three dates with Julia, she'd eaten off his plate last night and, though he knew it was an exercise in torture, he planned to blow the bachelor rules all to hell and spend the night with her tonight.

Leaving, when he knew their time was almost up, was out of the question. He didn't have the strength.

The new question, of course, would be if he had the strength to leave her tomorrow...

JULIA LAY PERFECTLY STILL and waited to see if Guy would respond to her "I'll miss you" comment, the one and only concession she intended to make on how very much he'd impacted her life in just a short time and how much she wished it wouldn't end. Five beats slid to ten and then she was forced to come to the unhappy conclusion that he was content to leave things the way they were.

Okay, she thought and released a slow breath.

She'd be fine, she told herself. The tightness in her chest would eventually go away and the heart which had lodged in her throat had to settle at some point. She felt her eyes sting, because things had been simply magical— better than anything she'd ever experienced and instinctively knew would ever experience again—but she determinedly blinked back the moisture and told herself to buck up.

Even knowing that they were through, Julia knew she wouldn't change a single thing about this week. No, that wasn't true. Realizing how precious their time would be together, she wouldn't have wasted that first day. One more day, she thought.

Who would have thought it would have been so important?

Of course, one day would lead to another and another and probably, given the tender emotion which rose in her chest every time she looked at Guy, she'd always want just one more day.

Her lips quirked. One more *now*.

If nothing else, he'd given that. Julia no

longer believed that she was a poor lover. Guy had made certain of that, taking her hard and fast, then soft and slow and always—always—wanting her. She could see it in those clear green eyes each and every time he looked at her. Desire, sexual hunger, always lurked in her pirate's gaze, Julia thought, smiling. Her shoulders shook with an unexpected chuckle. He'd certainly plundered the living hell out of her, that was for sure.

"What's so funny?" Guy wanted to know.

She giggled. "Nothing."

"That didn't sound like a nothing kind of giggle," he said suspiciously, drawing away so that he could look at her. "Come on," he cajoled. "Tell me."

Julia felt a blush was over her cheeks, but decided to share anyway. She rubbed a hand over his belly and sighed. "You know how I've told you that you remind me of a modern-day pirate?"

Guy chuckled. "Yes. You cited my disregard for rules, I believe."

"Right. Well, I was just laying here thinking about how fabulous being with you has been and— Well, what are pirates famous for?"

"Eye patches and peg legs."

"Smart-ass. Aside from that, what are they famous for?"

"Pillaging and plundering," he told her.

"Right. And I'd say you'd plundered the hell out of me, wouldn't you?"

Guy's neck arched back against the blanket and a loud laugh rumbled up his chest, vibrating her side. "Now that's an interesting analogy."

Julia smiled and pressed a kiss against his chest. "Well, you're an interesting guy."

"Thank you," he murmured. "You're pretty damned interesting yourself."

"I don't know about that," Julia said doubtfully. "But thanks for the compliment, anyway." She traced a jagged scar on his chest and frowned. "Did you get this while in the military?" she asked.

He stilled. "No. That one—all of them

actually—came from my old man. He was a mean bastard."

He said it glibly, as though getting beaten by his father had simply been a foregone conclusion. Horrified, Julia leaned up on one elbow so that she properly look at him. "Guy," she breathed softly, aching for the little boy he'd been. No wonder she hadn't been able to imagine him being small—he'd had that luxury snatched away from him at the hands of a parent, the ultimate betrayal.

He turned to look at her and offered a bracing smile. "No big deal," he said. "He was a drunk. He left when I was seventeen. Believe me, it was the best thing that ever happened to me or my mother."

"She couldn't protect you?"

He swallowed. "She tried."

Julia wanted to ask the obvious question— why didn't she leave a man who would beat her child? What in God's name had possessed her to stay? "Don't judge her," Guy said, evidently reading her line of thought. "He was good at being repentant and she was very religious. She did the best she could. She was a victim, too."

Julia knew that, but still…

"What about your family?" Guy wanted to know. "You've talked about your dad, but never mentioned your mother."

Julia rested her head against his shoulder once more. "Mom's mom," she said, smiling. "She's the poster child for plastic surgery and is swiftly running through Dad's retirement fund for the latest procedures, but he doesn't seem to mind."

"Plastic surgery, eh?" Guy said. He hummed under his breath. "You're not into that, are you?"

"No," Julia said, dragging the word out for emphasis.

He drew back to look at her again. Curiosity gleamed in his gaze. "Struck a nerve, did I?"

Julia chewed the inside of her cheek. "No." She sighed. "Let's just say my mother has never had any problem pointing out my imperfections."

"What?" he asked, seemingly outraged. "What the hell does she think is wrong with you? You're perfect."

Julia's lips slid into a grin, warmed by his comment. He had no idea what it meant to her, which made it all the more special. "I'm not perfect, but thank you."

"Stop arguing with me," he told her. "If I say you're perfect, then you're perfect, dammit. Anybody who says otherwise should have their eyes checked. Tell your mother to have laser surgery."

Julia chuckled. "She already has."

"What's she want to change about you?"

"My nose," Julia finally admitted. "It's big, I know. But it's mine and I'm not changing it."

Suddenly serious Guy leaned up so that he could look at her. "Julia, there is nothing—nothing—wrong with your nose. You are beautiful and what makes you so pretty is the fact that you don't realize how gorgeous you truly are." He bent down and pressed a gentle kiss on the tip of nose, causing her eyes to inexplicably water. "Don't ever change it."

"Thank you," Julia said, twining her arms around his neck and pulling him down to her mouth for a slow, deep kiss. She put every ounce of feeling she possessed into the melding of their mouths, the gratitude and desire, the hunger and the need. Gave it everything she had and then drew back.

Mossy green heavy lidded eyes stared back at her. "You should probably plunder the hell out of me again," Julia told him. *"Now."*

His lips quirked and humor danced in his gaze. "Shiver me timbers," he drawled, then fastened his mouth to hers.

# _11_

"THANKS FOR GIVING me another audience before you leave," Garrett said to both Julia and Guy. Looking beautiful but oddly tense, Guy watched Julia take the seat next to him. "I was interested in your final assessment and overall impression of the team. Ms. Beckam—" Garrett said, directing his attention to Julia "—how do you think the men responded to your portion of the class?"

Julia smiled. "Well, like most men they were a little concerned when they found out that I was a relationship therapist and I think they were afraid I was going to whip out the hand puppets or pass around a talking stick and make them share their feelings," she teased. "But once they realized that I was merely there to suggest ways to help them recognize, build and authenticate trust, they relaxed."

She'd hit the nail on the head, Guy thought. "Honestly, sir," Guy chimed in. "While I appreciated your original opinion on the matter, I was concerned, as well. However, Julia came right in and put the group at ease and I am certain that these men have benefited tremendously from her participation. She did a helluva job."

Julia smiled at him, evidently surprised at his praise. But it was true. She *had* done a fabulous job. She'd been organized, witty and well informed and the new team had responded to all of those things.

Hell, *he* had.

Garrett nodded, seemingly pleased. "Excellent," he said. "Would you be interested in doing this again, Ms. Beckam? Maybe on a longer scale?"

Julia nodded. "Certainly, sir. It was a pleasure."

"Thank you." His gaze slid to Guy. "Now,

if you don't mind, I'd like to speak to McCann alone."

Julia blinked. "Oh. Certainly."

She was leaving? Guy thought, suddenly panicked. Now? Oh, no. She couldn't leave. He needed to talk to her. There were things he needed to say. He wasn't entirely sure what yet, but he knew he couldn't let her walk away. "Don't leave before I get back," he murmured. "Please."

Catching his gaze, she looked a little wary, but nodded anyway.

Garrett waited until Julia had quietly let herself out of the room before speaking. "Okay, McCann, you've had a chance to look at Project Chameleon's replacement team. You've worked with them first hand. It's nut-cutting time. How do you think they're going to do? Do I need to retire? Or am I good for another few years?"

Guy blew out a breath and leaned forward in his chair. "They're green," he admitted. "But they're a good team, Colonel. And they're only going to get better. Each man brings something unique to the group and it's a good, solid dynamic. Furthermore, while they don't have the history that the first team had, they have been together enough to genuinely build a solid base." He leaned back once more. "I'd say you're career is safe for the time being."

Garrett deflated, his shoulders rounding under the weight of relief. "Thank God," he said. "The wife keeps yammering on about my joining the Garden Club and taking up photography."

"Photography?"

Garrett scowled. "She wants us to have a hobby we can share," he said grimly, as though it were a fate worse than death.

Guy suppressed a smile. "Oh."

"There are worse things, I'm sure, but I'm just not ready to end this chapter of my life." He paused and considered Payne thoughtfully. "I admire you, McCann, for having the courage to make a change. You and your friends." A long sigh leaked out of his lungs. "You stay in the same rut for so long that you lose the nerve to rattle the cart and clear the ditch. I love my job," he said. "I really do, but it's because I've never learned to do anything else."

Guy paused, touched by Garrett's unexpected confession and resulting praise. He'd always thought that he, Jamie and Payne had let Garrett down when they'd left the military. He'd never realized that the colonel had actually admired them for having the stones to make a change. Furthermore, he knew this little conversation hadn't been easy for Garrett and he truly appreciated that he'd taken him into his confidence.

Guy smiled at Garrett. "There's no need when you're so damned good at what you do, Colonel."

His face instantly creased into a broad smile. "Thanks, McCann. So what's next for you? I assume your security business is doing well?"

"Yes, sir."

"What about a personal level?" he asked

shrewdly. "Flanagan and Payne certainly haven't wasted any time finding a woman to keep the home fires burning."

An image of Julia leapt instantly to mind, making his chest alternately lighten and tighten. "I'm happy for them," Guy said, unwilling to answer the question, possibly because he was too terrified of the answer.

"Ms. Beckam is a wonderful girl. I've known her father for years, you know."

"She's fantastic."

"You compliment each other. You'd have beautiful children."

A chubby-cheeked baby girl with his eyes and Julia's golden hair materialized in his mind's eye, causing his breathing to hitch in his suddenly constricting throat.

Guy laughed nervously and stood. Time to exit. "Sir," he said with a finality that ended the conversation. "I'm sure I'll see you around."

The Colonel's eyes twinkled. "As it happens, you'll see me tomorrow."

"I'm sorry?"

"The wedding, McCann. Payne invited me."

Guy nodded. "Right." Considering it was Garrett's errand that made Payne and Emma's paths cross in the first place, it only stood to reason that Garrett would be invited. "Well."

"You should take Julia," Garrett suggested. "I suspect she and my granddaughter would be fast friends."

Guy merely smiled at him. "See you tomorrow, sir."

"Goodbye, McCann. Thank you."

Hand on the door knob, Guy paused. "You're welcome, sir."

And he meant it.

JULIA WAS SITTING ON THE front porch of duplex when Guy drove up. Her heart skipped a beat as she watched him slide out of the driver's seat and sidle up the sidewalk. She loved to watch him move. Loose and lean-hipped, he moved with a purposeful yet unhurried grace that was inherently sexy.

She didn't have any idea what he'd asked her to wait for—to say a proper goodbye, she imagined—but was secretly pleased that he had. She'd never gotten the chance—translate; hadn't drummed up the nerve—to address his feelings regarding Danny's death, but now that their time was at an end together, she knew she had to take her chance.

This was the end.

The end of their story.

He'd helped her, so it was time for her to reciprocate the gesture.

"Thanks for waiting on me," Guy said, looking curiously nervous.

She smiled softly at him, her heart melting. "You asked me, didn't you?" Julia paused. "What did Garrett have to say?"

Guy dropped heavily into the swing beside her and shot her a wry look. "You mean besides that you and I would make beautiful children?"

She gasped, stunned. "What?"

Guy grinned and shook his head. "He

fancies himself quite the matchmaker. Remember I told you that Jamie, Guy and I all owed him a favor?"

Julia nodded.

"Well, both of them met their significant other's while fulfilling Garrett's wishes. Jamie's married to the Colonel's granddaughter and Payne, well…Payne is getting married tomorrow, actually."

"Tomorrow? Wow," Julia said, trying to absorb it all.

"No," Guy laughed. "Here's the wow part—the bride doesn't know she's getting married yet."

Julia gaped. "You're kidding?"

"Payne's got it all arranged. Everything. You'd like him." He tugged playfully at her hair. "He's a planner like you."

"I'd like any friend of yours," she said. She batted her lashes at him. "You are an excellent judge of character."

Guy smiled. "You keep pretty good company yourself."

She felt her mouth slide into a grin. "It's improving."

"Go with me," he said suddenly, and from the startled expression on his face, quite unexpectedly.

"What?"

"To the wedding," he clarified. He paused and an endearingly nervous expression claimed his usually confident features. "Unless you already have plans tomorrow, that is. I would certainly understand if—"

"I'd love to," Julia said, inwardly squealing with joy. She'd go to the moon with him if it meant she'd have one more day.

Guy grinned and relief tugged at his shoulders. "Good. Wanna follow me home? You could stay at my place. Meet Bear," he said, pulling a shrug.

Julia feigned exaggerated delight. "You mean you like me enough to take me home to meet your dog?" She pressed a hand against her chest, pretending to be overcome.

"Hey," Guy teased. "I'll have you know that

no woman has ever met The Bear, much less been invited to spend the night at my house."

Julia stilled, absorbing the comment and what it meant. "Then I must be special."

He chuckled softly and shook his head. "Put your special ass in that car and let's go."

"You wanna give me the address?" Julia asked.

Having already stored his bags in the truck, Guy paused midway down the walk. "Address?"

"In case we get separated," Julia pointed out. Friday traffic in Atlanta was brutal and he'd mentioned that their offices and apartments were housed in midtown.

"Don't worry," he said, shooting her a smile. "I'm not going to leave you."

She knew what he meant—that he wasn't going to leave her behind on the highway—but that didn't keep her silly heart from doing a cartwheel and a somersault and a dizzy figure eight.

He reeled off his cell number and asked for hers. "No worries, okay?"

Julia nodded. "Not for now."

"Now?" Guy said, instantly seizing on their code word for back-bending balls-to-the-wall wild gorilla sex. "Did you say *now*?"

She chuckled. God, she was so falling for this man. "You know what I meant."

"I like my translation better." He back-tracked and nuzzled her cheek, sending a sparkler of pleasure dancing through her.

"I'll just bet you do."

"You do, too," Guy said matter of factly. His eyes danced with wicked humor. "I know you want me. Your eyes go all sleepy looking and your breathing gets shallow and sometimes, if I'm really lucky, I can see your nipples get hard beneath your shirt."

She felt a laugh break up in her throat. "That's nothing compared to what I see getting hard in your jeans when you want me," Julia pointed out.

He blinked innocently. "Can I help it if you're a pervert?"

"Pervert?" she said, feigning outrage.

"You didn't think I was a pervert last night when I was—"

"*Julia,*" he said, stopping her from finishing the graphic sentence.

"What?" she asked innocently.

Guy shook his head, seemingly at a loss. "I've created a monster." He heaved a long-suffering sigh and absently scratched his chest. "I suppose I'll simply have to keep you satisfied."

"Yes, well, we all make sacrifices," Julia pointed out wryly.

"I've explained that to you already," Guy told her. "Being with you is not a sacrifice—it's a pleasure. And it's all mine."

"It's mine, too," she murmured softly. "I don't know if anyone's ever told you before, but you're hot."

He chuckled, his eyes twinkling. "What am I going to do with you?"

Take me home and keep me, Julia thought. "That's what I wonder all the time," she said instead, giving his comment a completely different meaning.

"Come on," he said, nudging her forward. "And you can wonder all the way back to my apartment. And then I'll show you."

*Oy.* Now that sounded promising, Julia thought.

## *Atlanta*

"WELL, I'LL BE DAMNED," Payne breathed, staring the phone he'd just flipped closed.

"I hope not, darling," Emma told him. Bear lay sprawled across her lap, watching the proceedings with a look of sublime boredom. Guy would play hell getting that dog back from his soon-to-be wife, he thought. They'd bonded. So much so that the damned animal was calling the foot of their bed home.

Jamie frowned, going on alert and Audrey quirked a brow. "What's going on?" Jamie asked.

"He's bringing her back."

Jamie gaped. "The therapist?"

"Julia?" Emma squealed delightedly and she and Audrey shared a look of romantic feminine rapture that made Payne's head suddenly ache.

"Yes. He called to warn us of their arrival and has asked that we 'not leap to conclusions or gawk at her like a sideshow circus attraction.'"

Emma's brow furrowed. "Has he ever brought a girl here? To the apartment?"

Jamie shook his head. "Not that I'm aware of. Payne?"

"No," Payne said. "This is definitely a first."

Audrey rubbed a hand over her belly and smiled knowingly. "And it'll be the last, too. Mark my words. My grandfather has got a pretty good track record so far."

They certainly couldn't argue with that. He was two for two so far and if this thing with Guy ended up being the real thing, then they were all going to owe him again.

Big time.

Audrey and Jamie had already committed to naming their son after Garrett and while Payne and Emma had no immediate plans to start a family, he suspected that their child would end up with a similar namesake.

Of course, Emma was threatening to name their boy Robert E. Lee in honor of the pocket watch that had brought them together, but Payne held out hope that he could change her mind. He admired the Civil War hero as much as the next guy, but if had a son, he was inclined to name it after himself. His middle name, actually—Atticus.

He hadn't shared this particular longing with his fiancé yet, but one thing at a time, Payne told himself.

He should probably tell her about the wedding first.

# 12

JULIA SNUGGLED UP next to Guy and waited for her breathing to return to normal, which was difficult when she was still tingling from an intense orgasm. She flung an arm over her forehead and chuckled, savoring the moment of pure happiness.

They'd arrived back in Atlanta with plenty of time to meet—and ultimately have dinner with—Guy's friends, all of whom she instantly liked. Bear had given her the sniff of approval, going straight for her crotch when she'd walked into Guy's apartment, then he'd sniffed all over her, evidently following his master's scent.

Julia didn't know what she'd expected Guy's apartment to be like, but the modern contemporary blended with traditional antiques wasn't it. Naturally he'd spent the majority of his decorating budget on electronics—a big screen TV, an expensive stereo system as well as the newest entertainment toys. "PlayStation?" she'd teased, quirking a brow at him.

"Don't knock it 'til you try it, baby. I'll take you on in Ultra Mega Smackdown any day."

Sweet Lord. Everything about him—even his video games—was ultimately endearing.

"What are you thinking about?" Guy asked.

She chuckled. "I thought that was supposed to be my line?"

"Smart-ass."

"Do you really want to know?"

"I wouldn't have asked otherwise."

"I was thinking about you and your games and how I find you completely adorable."

He sighed, evidently pleased. "Adorable is nice…but I prefer sexy."

Julia rolled closer and pressed a kiss against his naked chest. "We've already established that." She sighed. "I liked your friends," she said. "They're great."

This time it was his turn to chuckle. "And they liked you, too. Audrey and Emma both made sure to take me aside and sing your praises, though Emma was a bit confused over what you looked like."

"What? Why?"

"She thought you had red hair."

"Red hair? But—" Then it hit her and mortification swiftly followed. "The mug shot," she breathed. "I knew Payne had seen it, but I didn't realize he'd passed it around." Julia rubbed a hand over her face and laughed helplessly. "Quick. Find me a hole."

Guy laughed and hauled her up closer against him. "You don't need a hole, goofball. They thought it was funny."

"It was humiliating." A thought struck. "You have to delete that from your phone."

"Okay."

He'd agreed too readily, making Julia suspicious. "You don't mind?"

"No." She heard the smile in his voice. "I've already e-mailed it to my computer."

She whacked him playfully. "You're horrible. Have you ever been arrested?" Julia asked. "I think I should have a mug shot of you."

"Sorry to disappoint you, but no."

"Really?" she asked.

"You sound surprised," Guy said, chuckling.

"Well, you are a badass," she reminded him. "Most badasses usually end up in jail at one point or another."

"This one kept his nose clean."

She hummed under her breath, feigning disappointment. "Okay. I'll simply have to think of something else."

Guy's laugh rumbled next to her ear. "You do that."

"Does Emma know about the wedding yet?"

"Nope."

Julia frowned, considering things. "I don't get it. How is he getting her into the wedding gown tomorrow?"

"Pictures," Guy said, sighing softly.

"Pictures? Already?"

"He's a planner, remember?"

"Wow," Julia said, impressed. "He's really thought of everything, hasn't he?"

Guy let go a soft breath. "He's not called The Specialist for nothing."

"The Specialist?"

"His nickname."

"Oh. Did you all have nicknames?"

He chuckled again, the sound intimate and sexy between them. "Mostly we just called each other bastards."

Julia laughed. "Men," she said. "And guys say women are complicated."

A soft sigh stuttered out of Guy's mouth. "Jamie and I didn't have a nickname, but I guess Danny did. We always called him Danny Boy. You know, like the song."

"I love that song," Julia said softly.

"Like Jamie, Danny was Irish so it fit. Both of them had Irish grandmothers."

Here was her chance, Julia thought. If she

was ever going to have an opening to try and help him see the truth, this was it.

Still, she hesitated, not altogether certain he wanted to hear her opinion on the subject. Oh, well, Julia thought. There were lots of things that people didn't necessarily want to hear, but that didn't change the fact that they *needed* to hear it.

"Guy, there's something I've been wanting to talk to you about," she began.

"What?"

"Danny's death. You know it's not your fault, don't you?"

She felt him tense beside her. "Julia, I know that you're only trying to help, but this is something that you don't know anything about. Please," he said, his voice hardening. "Leave it."

Just as she expected. She released a shaky breath. "Actually, that's not true. I listened when you told the new team about the mission when Danny was killed."

"They got the abbreviated version. Let it

go." His voice rang with a warning she knew she should heed, and yet curiously couldn't.

"You said you were ambushed. If you were ambushed, then how could it be your fault?"

Guy sprang up from the bed. "What the hell are you doing?" he demanded. "I don't want to talk about this with you. I'm not going to."

"You helped me," she said simply. "I want to help you and I think I can."

"Bullshit," Guy snapped. "If I want your help, then I'll ask for it. This is none of your damned business. Don't try to get inside my head and start mucking around with your therapist talk, Julia. It's insulting."

She blinked, taken aback by the attack. "I just—"

"Just nothing," he interrupted. "You don't know, dammit," he said, striding away from her.

"I know that if you were ambushed then it couldn't have been your fault, that it hadn't been preventable. I know that you're drowning in your own grief and punishing yourself for something that you didn't have any control over. And I know that as long as you keep blaming yourself, you're insulting your friend."

He whirled on her. "Insulting my friend?" he asked in a dangerously low voice.

"His memory," Julia clarified, terrified that she'd crossed a line, but too far over to stop now.

She watched Guy go dangerously still and knew that she'd gone too far. "Guy, listen to me. I—"

"I can see that this was a mistake," he said. "It's late. I'll call you a cab and have your car returned to you tomorrow."

*What? No!* "Guy, please—"

"I'll wait in the living room while you get dressed and collect your things." And without another backward glance, he turned and walked out of the room.

Out of her life.

So that was it, then, Julia thought resignedly, her heart breaking. Tears burned the backs of her lids and the ache in her chest threatened to choke the life right out of her, but she refused to cry. This had been inevitable. She'd known that. What was that old saying again? When you're dumb you've got to be tough.

And she felt like the ultimate fool.

"WHERE'S JULIA?"

The next person who asked him that was going to get coldcocked, friend or not.

Guy glanced at Jamie and felt his jaw harden. "I sent her home."

"Home?" he asked, surprised. "Why?"

"She started psychoanalyzing me and I didn't care for it," Guy said, inserting enough warning into his voice to dissuade further conversation.

Jamie smiled knowingly. "Let me guess. She wanted to talk about Danny."

He snorted. "She doesn't know what the hell she's talking about, dammit, and yet she keeps insisting that—"

"—that it's not your fault," Jamie finished. "Audrey did the same thing to me. I thought I told you that."

Guy shook his head. "No." He knew that Jamie had come back from Audrey's camp a changed man, but had just always assumed that he'd made his own peace.

He got the grim suspicion he was about to learn otherwise.

Jamie laughed, remembering. "She hammered away at me the entire week I was there, man. Like a dog with a bone."

"What did you do?"

"Changed the subject. Distracted her with sex. Walked away." He smiled. "Then she rowed me out into the lake—in late September, no less—and set in on me, thinking that she'd trapped me, that I'd *have* to talk to her."

Guy felt his jaw drop. Little Audrey? Wow. Now that took balls. He'd be hard pressed to try and trap Jamie his own self. "What did you do?"

Jamie laughed. "What the hell do you think I did? I told her that I was a friggin' Ranger, by God, and I dove out of the boat and started swimming for shore."

Guy laughed, not the least bit surprised. He could certainly see Jamie doing just that. "What did she do?"

"That was the amazing part," Jamie said. He searched the crowded reception room until his gaze landed on his wife and a wondering expression came over his face. "She dove in after me."

"Really?" Guy asked, stunned.

Jamie nodded. "And I know you don't want to hear this, partner, but hearing her out changed my life. For the better, as I'm sure you've noticed." His gaze turned speculative. "Women think differently from men, see things in a way that guys oftentimes can't grasp. Pride and grief have a way of eroding logic." He paused. "I hope you didn't run her off because she was trying to tell you that Danny's death wasn't your fault. Because it wasn't."

Him, too? Guy thought. Dammit to hell, why couldn't everyone leave him alone and let him grieve the way he wanted to, the way he deserved to. "I was unit commander," Guy said harshly. "And I lost a man."

"And I was supposed to have his back and I missed it."

"You didn't miss it—you were ambushed. How the hell were you supposed to prepare for that?" Guy demanded.

Jamie smiled knowingly. "Exactly."

"I orchestrated the mission," Payne said, having walked up on the tail end of the conversation. "We used my strategy. Technically, it could be my fault, as well."

"It's your wedding day," Guy said, disgusted at the tag team effort the two of them had going on. "We shouldn't be talking about this."

"You're wrong," Payne said. "We should have talked about it a long time ago."

"Danny was our friend, Guy, and we miss him, but he would be miserable—insulted even—if he knew that we were blaming ourselves for a risk that came with the job."

Insulted? Guy thought, remembering Julia's comment from last night. An uneasy tingling started in the small of his back and settled in his stomach.

"He'd hate it," Payne said. "And the best

way to honor his memory is to stop blaming ourselves and celebrate the life he lived, not perpetually mourn the one he lost."

Jamie clapped him on the back. "He wouldn't want this, man. I don't want to get into your business, but don't you think that if Julia was special enough to bring home to meet us, then she's worth fighting for?"

"You flew off the handle and ran that mouth, didn't you," Payne said. He tsked under his breath. "Emma and Audrey said that it's obvious that she's crazy about you. You can fix it."

He sure as hell would like to know how, Guy thought, feeling the first quickening of dread and misery unwinding in his gut.

*You helped me. I want to help you.*

And he'd shut her out and belittled and berated her for her trouble.

He was an ass, Guy decided. A stupid, miserable ass.

"Is there anything we can do?" Payne asked.

"Go on your honeymoon," Guy told him.

"It's bad enough I've dumped this shit on you at your wedding."

Payne smiled at his bride, so in love it made Guy's own chest ache. "It went off without a hitch."

Jamie snorted. "You wouldn't allow a hitch."

And there was that, Guy thought. "Look, guys… I just want you to know—"

"We already do," Payne told him.

Jamie grinned. "Hell, we're friends, aren't we?"

The best ones, Guy thought, humbled and touched and altogether blessed with their part in his life. He'd always known it, of course, but never had it been made more clear to him than in this instant.

"You don't have to hang around here," Payne told him. "Emma and I are leaving shortly." He smiled at him. "Go get your girl."

Payne certainly knew what he was talking about when it came to that. They'd all fallen into the car and tracked down Emma for him after she'd left.

Guy rubbed the back of his neck. "I—"

"Go get her, Guy," Jamie insisted. "She's the one for you. I knew it the instant I saw her."

He had, too, Guy thought. And he'd been terrified ever since.

"Any ideas on how you're going to win her back?" Jamie asked. "You'll need a plan."

Guy wracked his brain, knew that it was going to take something more than a mere "I'm dumb ass please forgive me" to settle things between them. Besides, Julia deserved better. She deserved a grand gesture, something that she would know he'd done just for her.

And then it hit him. "Is her file still in the office?"

Payne nodded.

"Good," he said, suddenly energized with a purpose. "I need a pirate costume and if she doesn't come bail me out of jail, one of you bastards will have to do it." He looked at Jamie. "It'll have to be you, Flanagan. Payne's going to be busy."

Jamie gaped and Payne's jaw went slack. "A pirate costume?"

"Bail you out of jail?"

Guy grinned at both of them, then congratulated Payne and slapped him on the arm. "Bye, guys. I've got a treasure to find."

And her name was Julia.

# *13*

CHUNKY MONKEY OR ROCKY ROAD? Julia wondered, staring morosely into her freezer. What the hell. She'd have both. She pulled both containers out and promptly filled a bowl. Chocolate therapy, she thought, shuffling back into the living room. What else would a shrink need?

Besides a lobotomy and a new heart?

*Why, why, why* had she kept pushing him when she knew he'd been getting angrier and angrier? Why couldn't she have done what he asked and simply let it go?

She knew why—she knew that he was hurting and she wanted to take care of him. But you couldn't take care of someone who didn't want to admit anything was wrong, and if she'd merely played along, she could still be with him, laughing and nuzzling and having wild, wonderful sex.

She'd still be with him, would have had another day, and then maybe another.

More *nows*.

If she'd only been patient, then she might have been able to bring him around by degrees. As a therapist, she knew this, but something told her that Guy McCann's head was too thick to respond to that kind of treatment—it would have to be cracked open, emptied out, and reassembled, she decided, the idea drawing a small sad smile.

Unfortunately, she didn't have the where-withal to do it.

He'd basically kicked her out and she'd left because she'd been hurt and mortified by his rejection.

Her only consolation was that she knew that she was right and she'd driven her own damned car home.

Call her a cab, my ass. As though she were

a hooker he'd met on the street that he could conveniently ship off at a moment's notice. Logic told her that he'd been concerned for her safety, but her heart had been aching too hard to accommodate clear thinking. She'd—

Julia stilled as a noise snagged her attention and she listened closely. What was that? It was coming from the living room window.

She carefully set her bowl aside, fear making her pulse leap into overdrive. Another sound, this one more insistent, reached her ears and in a nanosecond she realized what was happening.

Someone was trying to break into her window.

Shaking so hard she could barely dial, Julia snagged her cordless phone and quietly moved to the kitchen where she promptly dialed 911. "What do I do?" Julia asked, terrified.

"Stay on the line until the authorities get there," the operator told her.

"Shouldn't I run? Aren't I trapped in the house? I—"

Her living-room window shattered and she heard someone swear from outside. Julia frowned. The voice sounded oddly familiar. "Hold on a minute," Julia said. "I'm going to check something out."

"Ma'am, you don't need to do that. Wait for the authorities. They should be there any minute now. Ma'am? Ma'am?"

Julia peered around the door frame and watched as a leg encased in blousy black pants angled in through her broken window. "Son of a bitch…" she heard the intruder mumble. He braced an arm inside the frame and it was then that she noticed the shirt—white, equally blousy…almost like a pirate's outfit. "…from a friggin' stallion to gelding if I'm not careful," she heard him say. "Honestly."

Julia blinked, astonished. "Guy?"

He banged his head against the windowsill and swore. "Damn it all to hell— Julia?"

"Ma'am? Ma'am?" came the insistent operator. "What's going on? Do you know your attacker?"

She opened her mouth, closed it, then opened it again. "He's not my attacker," she said. "It's fine. I know this man."

Sirens sounded in the distance and to Julia's astonishment, Guy actually looked pleased with the prospect of getting arrested. "Oh, good. They're almost here." He grimaced at the window. "Sorry about that. The door would have been too casy."

"What the hell are you doing?" she demanded. "I could have shot you."

"But you don't have a gun," he pointed out, looking at her hands to makc sure.

"But I could have! What the hell is wrong with you? Why didn't you knock like a normal person?"

"Because I'm trying to get arrested," he said, seemingly exasperated with her because she wasn't following his cockeyed logic.

Her eyes bugged. "Get arrested? Why?"

"So that I can give you a mug shot." He paused and lowered his voice. "Along with my heartfelt apologies."

The pirate suit, the mug shot. Julia felt a wild laugh break up in her throat. "Have you lost—"

The police roared into her driveway cutting off what she was about to say. Julia's gaze swung from him to the blue lights flashing outside and stifled a groan. "Hold on," she said. "Let me go take care of this."

"No!" Guy insisted. "You have to press charges."

He'd clearly lost his mind. "What?"

"You've got to press charges. For the mug shot." That endearingly crooked smile curled his lips. "And then I was hoping that you would come bail me out."

She knew she kept repeating him, but she couldn't seem to help herself. It was too much. Unbelievable. "Bail you out?"

He nodded. "I'd appreciate it. And I want you to forgive me, too, if it's not too much trouble."

Her heart melted like a pat of butter over a warm bun. "*Guy.*"

A knock sounded at her door. "Police!"

"You don't have to do this," she said quickly. "I forgive you."

"I know I don't have to, Julia…but I want to. For you. Because you're special."

Uniformed officers burst into the room. "Freeze!" They tackled Guy to the floor and in short order had him cuffed. Rather than looking put out or frightened, he looked downright pleased with himself.

"You want to follow us to the station, ma'am?"

"Sure. How long before I can bail him out?"

The officer blinked. "What?"

"How long before I can bail him out?" she repeated. What? Had she stuttered?

Thoroughly confused, the cop looked from Guy to Julia and back again. "If you're just going to bail him out, what's the point in pressing charges?"

"It's complicated," Julia said, her gaze tangling with Guy's.

An hour later, Julia watched Guy stroll across the parking lot toward her car. The pirate outfit ballooned around him and for a second he looked like the genuine article. She leaned her head out the window of her car. "Need a lift?"

Smiling, mug shot in hand, Guy climbed in beside her and handed the picture over. "Not bad, considering they took my eye patch," he said.

Her heart pounding wildly, Julia nodded. Her mouth parched at the unbelievable gesture. "It's nice. Thank you."

"I owe you an apology," he said without preamble. "I was an ass."

"You are, but I knew that already. I should have left you alone."

"Don't you get it? That's why I'm here." He reached over and ran the pad of his thumb over her bottom lip. "I never want you to leave me alone. Call me an ass, tell me to go to hell, but don't ever leave me again, even if I'm trying to run you off." He paused, swallowed tightly. "I need you."

Her eyes misted, recognizing the gesture

for what it was. In his own roundabout way her badass former Ranger, modern-day pirate was trying to tell her that he loved her.

He was botching it up, of course, but…

"I love you, too," Julia told him, chuckling softly.

He smiled and breathed a significant sigh of relief.

"And do you know what I'd really like you to do?" she asked him.

"Name it."

"I want you to love me…*now*."

That slow wicked smile she'd come to love spread across those sinfully crafted lips and he laughed softly, the sound eddying through her, vibrating over every nerve in her body. "Baby, just say the word," Guy told her, then his mouth found hers and sealed the promise with a kiss.

# _Epilogue_

_Three months later…_

"ARE WE TOO LATE?" Julia asked, hurrying into the maternity waiting area. Guy trailed along behind her, content to watch her move.

Emma shook her head. "Nope. No baby yet. Jamie's in there with her."

"And you can bet he's a nervous wreck," Payne drawled, doodling his fingers on his wife's upper arm. "Just like I will be six months from now when Emma delivers our first."

Julia's gaze swung to Emma's and she gasped, then squealed with delight as Emma, misty eyed, confirmed her husband's announcement. Guy smiled and looked to Payne for confirmation. The Specialist nodded once.

"Didn't waste any time, did you?" Guy asked. "Congratulations. You'll make a fine father."

Julia tugged at his arm, pressed her lips up against his ear. "You will, too," she whispered.

Guy drew back and blinked. "Do you mean—"

A gorgeous grin spread across her lips and her eyes twinkled with delight. "I do."

Emma looked from Julia to Guy and back again. Her eyes widened. "Oh, my God. Are you?"

"February eleventh," Julia told her.

Impossibly, Emma's eyes widened farther. "Mine, too," she breathed.

Payne chuckled and looked at Guy. "Sounds like someone else didn't waste any time on my honeymoon," he teased. "Congratulations."

"Meet Daniel Garrett Flanagan," Jamie announced proudly from the doorway, Colonel Garrett at his side.

"My great-grandson," the colonel said unnecessarily, beaming from ear to ear.

Emma and Audrey instantly moved into

place so that they could get a better look at the baby, but Guy and Payne hung back and the three of them shared a smile. An understanding passed between them, the unspoken communication that they'd used for years. Guy didn't have to hear Jamie's thoughts to know that he was more proud of his son than he'd ever been of anything in his life. Nor did he have to hear Payne say that Emma completed him, when one look at the two of them together told any fool that.

And as for himself, Guy thought. Well, he had Julia…and he wanted her *now* as much as he wanted her forever.

\* \* \* \* \*

# *Decadent*

## *by*

### *Suzanne Forster*

RUN, ALLY! Don't be fooled by him. He's evil. Don't let him touch you!

But as the forbidding figure came through the mists toward her, Ally knew she couldn't run. His features burned with dark malevolence, and his physical domination of everything around him seemed to hold her like a net.

She'd heard the tales. She knew all about the Wolverton legend and the ghost that haunted The Willows, an elegant old mansion lost by Micha Wolverton nearly a hundred years ago. According to folklore, the estate was stolen from the Wolvertons, and Micha was killed, trying to reclaim it. His dying vow was to be reunited with the spirit of his beloved wife, who'd taken her life for reasons no one would speak of, except in whispers. But Ally had never put much stock in the fantasy. She didn't believe in ghosts.

Until now—

She still didn't understand what was happening. The figure had materialized out of the mist that lay thick on the damp cemetery soil. A cool breeze and silvery moonlight had played against the ancient stone of the crypts surrounding her, until they joined the mist, causing his body to thicken and solidify right before her eyes. That was when she realized she'd seen this man before. Or thought she had, at least.

His face was familiar…so familiar, yet she couldn't put it together. Not with him looming so near. She stepped back as he approached.

"Don't be afraid," he said. His voice wasn't what she expected. It didn't sound as if it were coming from beyond the grave. It was deep and sensual. Commanding.

"Who are you?" she managed.

"You should know. You summoned me."

"No, I didn't." She had no idea what he was talking about. Two minutes ago, she'd been crouching behind a moss-covered crypt, spying on the mansion that had once been The Willows, but was now Club Casablanca. And then this—

If he was Micah, he might be angry that she was trespassing on his property. "I'll go," she said. "I won't come back. I promise."

"You're not going anywhere."

Words snagged in her throat. "Wh-why not? What do you want?"

"If I wanted something, Ally, I'd take it. This is about need."

His words resonated as he moved within inches of her. She tried to back away, but her feet were useless. "And you need something from me?"

"Good guess." His tone burned with irony. "I need lips, soft and surrendered, a body limp with desire."

"My lips, my bod—?"

"Only yours."

"Why? Why me?" This couldn't be Micha.

He didn't want any woman but Rose. He'd died trying to get back to her.

"Because you want that, too," he said.

Wanted what? A ghost of her own? She'd always found the legend impossibly romantic, but how could he have known that? How could he know anything about her? Besides, she'd sworn off inappropriate men, and what could be more inappropriate than a ghost? She shook her head again, still not willing to admit the truth. But her heart wouldn't play along. It clattered inside her chest. The mere thought of his kiss, his touch, terrified her. This wildness, it was fear, wasn't it?

When his fingertips touched her cheek, she flinched, expecting his flesh to be cold, lifeless. It was anything but that. His skin was smooth and hot, gentle, yet demanding. And while his dark brown eyes were filled with mystery and wonder, there was a sensitivity about them that threatened to disarm her if she looked too deeply.

"These lips are mine," he said, as if stating

a universal fact that she was helpless to avoid. In truth, it was just that. She couldn't stop him. And she didn't want to.

\* \* \* \* \*

# FREE

## 2 BOOKS AND A SURPRISE GIFT!

We would like to take this opportunity to thank you for reading this Mills & Boon® book by offering you the chance to take TWO more specially selected titles from the Blaze® series absolutely FREE! We're also making this offer to introduce you to the benefits of the Mills & Boon® Reader Service™—

> ★ **FREE home delivery**
> ★ **FREE gifts and competitions**
> ★ **FREE monthly Newsletter**
> ★ **Books available before they're in the shops**
> ★ **Exclusive Reader Service offers**

Accepting these FREE books and gift places you under no obligation to buy; you may cancel at any time, even after receiving your free shipment. Simply complete your details below and return the entire page to the address below. You don't even need a stamp!

**YES!** Please send me 2 free Blaze books and a surprise gift. I understand that unless you hear from me, I will receive 4 superb new titles every month for just £3.10 each, postage and packing free. I am under no obligation to purchase any books and may cancel my subscription at any time. The free books and gift will be mine to keep in any case.

K7ZEE

Ms/Mrs/Miss/Mr.........................................Initials .................................
**BLOCK CAPITALS PLEASE**

Surname ..........................................................................................

Address ............................................................................................

.......................................................................................................

.............................................Postcode ...............................................

Send this whole page to:

The Reader Service, FREEPOST CN81, Croydon, CR9 3WZ

Offer valid in UK only and is not available to current Mills & Boon Reader Service™ subscribers to this series. Overseas and Eire please write for details. We reserve the right to refuse an application and applicants must be aged 18 years or over. Only one application per household. Terms and prices subject to change without notice. Offer expires 31st January 2008. As a result of this application, you may receive offers from Harlequin Mills & Boon and other carefully selected companies. If you would prefer not to share in this opportunity please write to The Data Manager at PO Box 676, Richmond, TW9 1WU.

Mills & Boon® is a registered trademark owned by Harlequin Mills & Boon Limited.
Blaze® is being used as a registered trademark owned by Harlequin Mills & Boon Limited.
The Mills & Boon® Reader Service™ is being used as a trademark.